DEADLY ASSAULT

Casca and Dave charged straight at the bridge. The single soldier left standing fired at them, but his shot went wide, and he was still working the bolt of his rifle when Casca's bayonet opened his gut.

"Messy way to kill," he grumbled as he jerked the bayonet free, and the German fell into the puddle of his own blood and intestines.

The Casca series
by Barry Sadler

CASCA:

THE TRENCH SOLDIER

#21

BARRY SADLER

J

JOVE BOOKS, NEW YORK

CASCA #21: THE TRENCH SOLDIER

A Jove Book / published by arrangement with
the author

PRINTING HISTORY
Jove edition / February 1989

ISBN: 0-515-09931-7

Jove Books are published by The Berkley Publishing Group,
200 Madison Avenue, New York, New York 10016.
The name ''JOVE'' and the ''J'' logo
are trademarks belonging to Jove Publications, Inc.

PRINTED IN THE UNITED STATES OF AMERICA

10 9 8 7 6 5 4 3 2 1

THE TRENCH SOLDIER

CHAPTER ONE

Rufus Casterton limped painfully along the snow-covered, dirty street shivering uncontrollably in the freezing, wet wind. It was April, but spring comes late to London. With every step the frozen stones of the pavement struck fresh chills into his feet through the paper-thin soles of his worn-out shoes. The right sole leaked and sucked in ice-cold water every time it touched the ground.

He wore the uniform of the men who had been described by an obscure poet as "the army of the rear," the tattered and dirty unemployed who were to be found on the streets of every English city—greasy cloth cap, a suit stained and crumpled from being slept in through all weathers, and a thin cotton shirt that did little to keep the keen wind from his chest.

At every corner there stood a bobby. Casterton would have gladly killed any one of them just for his clothes. Stout boots that kept the feet snug in woolen socks, a uniform of warm wool serge topped by a shiny, black helmet, and all protected by an oilskin cape. Neither rain, hail, sleet, nor snow could penetrate the London bobby's protection against the city's vile climate.

But Casterton knew only too well there was no way to get at one of these constables. All night long they marched the streets of the city, each assigned to a section four blocks by four blocks, forbidden to leave any one street until he had sighted the next constable on his adjoining beat.

At no time was any one bobby farther than four blocks

1

from a comrade, and should the other peeler fail to appear
as expected, a single shrill blast would bring running every
copper within earshot.

The system worked so well that the rich burghers of
London slept soundly and unconcerned, their doors closed
more against the foul weather than in fear of malefactors.
Servant girls and porters were sent on errands for their
masters and unhesitatingly trod the gaslit streets at all hours
of the night.

The horror of "Jack the Ripper" had been quickly forgotten once the old Queen's insane son, the Duke of Clarence, generally deemed responsible, had been discreetly
locked away. The attacks had promptly ceased, and prosti-
tutes again plied their trade free of the fear of sudden attack
by a well-dressed gent carrying a respectable doctor's bag
full of surgeon's instruments.

But the death of the old Queen, perhaps hastened by her
son's lunacy and the dawn of the Twentieth Century, had
ushered in an era of hardship never previously known in
the small island that ruled the world. The mad Clarence had
died in a lunatic asylum, and another son, the extravagant,
luxury loving Edward VII had succeeded the old Queen on
the throne.

The British Empire had grown to fantastic proportions,
her dominion stretching from the frozen Arctic wastes of
Canada in the north to some of the southernmost islands of
the planet, the Falklands and New Zealand. From London
the rule of Britannia extended east and west so that British
ships could circle the globe by the "All Red Route" and
never be obliged to put into a foreign port. And in every
port an English gentleman would feel at home. There would
be the Union Jack flying, troops, no matter of what race or
creed or color, in British uniforms, women who, if not
naturally frigid, acted so in order to seem more British, and
the most uneatable food.

India and South Africa were British. China and Egypt
were not but were ruled from London all the same. The

Chinese had surrendered Hong Kong, and even on mainland China the Collector of Customs was a British official. Egypt was a British ''protectorate.'' Greece was a dependent kingdom, its ruler of British blood. The old Queen's sons and grandsons sat on every throne from Moscow to Sweden. The British royal family, the House of Hanover, was of German blood, but now, like almost every royal family in the world, it served England.

India was a British colony as was Burma. Siam paid tribute, while Tibet was a vassal state. At an enormous cost in lives, Afghanistan had repelled three British invasions and was almost unique in Asia in remaining truly independent.

The world was largely at peace. From Nepal to Nova Scotia, a *Pax Britannica* held sway as the *Pax Romana* had in the time of Christ.

The British Empire had no farthest limit on the planet. No river, not even the vastest oceans, bounded its sway. And the peoples of the far-flung dominions, protectorates, spheres of influence, and possessions of the empire were so ready to supply troops for their own domination that the Imperial Crown had no need of mercenaries and even disdained a standing home army of any size.

The result was that soldiering was not only a poorly paid occupation—it was one that scarcely existed. The depressed economy at home and the unlimited supply of ever-willing-to-fight Irish ensured that the British Army never went short of a man.

And experienced mercenary that he was, Casterton was not fool enough to look for employment in the armies of Great Britain's few ambitious enemies. Not only were they certain of defeat, they could not afford decent pay.

While outside the British Empire the world was largely at peace and peaceful, too. Great Britain had treaties with her traditional enemies, Russia and France, that kept the other European powers from adventuring against any of them. The few conflicts that did break out between the smaller states of Europe, or even Asia, were quickly settled by the diplomatic intervention of British ambassadors who mediated the quarrels like kindly uncles presiding over nursery squabbles.

Except for France, which had an elected president, there was a noble ass in the person of a king, prince or czar on all the thrones of Europe and Asia, from Moscow to Tehran to Tonga. And most of them were children or grandchildren of Victoria and her German consort or were puppets who owed their crowns to the British.

But if the rule of the Crown promised peace, it also guaranteed poverty. The seizure of the peoples' common lands through the Enclosure Acts had made paupers of England's once prosperous yeoman class, and a similar fate had been exported to all of the colonies. All power emanated from London, and all wealth flowed there. The riches of most of the world poured into London and into a very few pockets.

The small handful of gentry who owned the British Empire had instituted a form of democracy to keep at bay the dangerous revolutionary ideas of America and France. The House of Lords held only the titled nobility while their younger brothers, cousins, and nephews sat in the House of Commons where the Prime Ministership, albeit through the process of the ballot box, passed from father to son and uncle to nephew. The common people had no say at all in the doings of Parliament and expected none. Although every Londoner knew the stately buildings, Parliament was a mysterious and exclusive territory as remote as the moon to most Englishman.

There were few jobs to be had, all of them bad. Germany, France, Italy, and the U.S.A. had come late to the Industrial Revolution, having seen and avoided the worst of England's mistakes. And now, especially in America, men of enterprise were proving their worth with new ideas and products while getting rich in the process. Germany had leaped ahead in chemicals and petroleum derivatives and was planning a railroad from Baghdad to Berlin which would bring Iraq's oil to Germany more quickly and more cheaply than British ships.

In England enterprise was a dangerous word. Men of capital ruled industry and commerce, reluctantly using, buying up, or marrying their daughters to the occasional man of enterprise who could not otherwise be contained. Some, like Tommy Lipton, a fo'c'sle-hand-come-tea-merchant (some said opium runner), had even been granted (some said sold) a knighthood. But for all that, the old, inbred families and their old ways had ensured that British industry and commerce had stagnated for a quarter century.

The imperious monarch, Edward VII, who had forced Prime Minister Asquith to kiss his hands, was succeeded in 1910 by King George V, who although less inclined to parade the enjoyment of his enormous wealth, had effected no change for the better in the lives of the subjects of the British Crown.

The millionaire confectioner, Rowntree, in order to establish a level of payment for his own employees, had defined a minimum level for household needs and found that a third of England's population failed to reach it. In all weathers the Thames embankment was crammed with the unemployed sleeping out. The jails were crowded. In South Wales reluctant miners were forced to work in the pits at the point of army guns.

Casterton very much regretted leaving China where he had been a much respected and well rewarded functionary in the government of Sun Yat-sen and his warlord Chiang Kai Shek. At first things had gone well for him in London, but a chance meeting in the Strand with a retired British China Company colonel had forced him to find his new name and to go into hiding amongst the lowest levels of the city's poor. Colonel Braithwaite had no love for him and had not forgotten either the lieutenant that Casterton had publicly executed in Hong Kong or the parcel of gold, opium, and other valuables that was still unaccounted for and had severely compromised Braithwaite's career. Casterton had been sentenced to hang for the death of the lieutenant and would receive the same sentence for the theft and for his desertion, though the crimes had taken place more than ten years previously.

Inside England anybody who could pass for an Englishman could call himself by any name he chose, and the man who, as Casca Rufius Longinus, had once served in the legions of Augustus Caesar had settled on Rufus Casterton, a variant of the name on his American passport.

Not that it made any difference if he were called Cassius, Casterton, or Casca. As one of the capital's huge army of starving bums, he was invisible. Colonel Braithwaite would not deign to so much as glance in the direction of such a derelict should he pass him in the street.

The late snow had turned to sleet and the two mixed to a muddy, freezing slush on the cobblestones. Casca hunched into his thin clothes and pressed against the wall to get out of the way of a cab that was turning out of the driveway of a mansion. As it passed Casca heard the passenger shout the address.

A small crowd of derelicts set off after the cab, jostling each other as they ran, the fleetest and toughest quickly getting to the front of the mob, panting along almost in reach of the rear step while the others fanned out behind him in a wake of tattered humanity.

Casca ran down the street to the right. He would have to run an extra two blocks, but he knew he could manage that and still win the race. He suffered the pangs of hunger as much as any bum on the streets of London, but the curse that had kept him alive for two thousand years continued to rebuild his muscular body even when it was fed only on scraps.

He raced down into Oxford Street by Marble Arch and

through Portman Square with its fine houses to Baker Street and Regent's Park to meet the cab as it came clattering onto the cobblestones of Park Road.

The sorry crew running after it had diminished to half a dozen and they were now strung out in a long line, the same man in the lead, but now well behind the cab and falling farther back with every stride.

Casca ran briefly alongside him and tripped him deftly. The big man went down heavily, his face hitting the cobbles with a resounding whack.

A moment later the cab drew up at the street door of a large house, and Casca opened the cab door and stood back, cap in hand.

A swell stepped out, dropped a penny into the cap and strolled to where a servant was opening the front door. The cab driver climbed down to rub the sweat from his horse before walking him back to the cabman's shelter in Harrow Road.

The losers in the race were now bunched together, helping up the man Casca had tripped. Their mood and their looks were threatening, but the fallen one's nose was broken, and he was in no shape for a fight. Without him the others would not pit their puny strengths against Casca. He crossed the street and walked back past them on the opposite sidewalk ignoring their curses and jibes.

He had the price of a bun. Now, if he could just get another half-penny, he could enjoy it with a cup of tea. The prospect warmed his belly and his step was almost jaunty as he headed back toward the cabman's shelter.

In Baker Street a door opened and a butler stepped out into the street. Through the open door Casca could see a young woman wearing a huge, ungainly hat and a thin shawl waiting nervously in the hall.

"You there," the butler called to him, "ha'penny for a cab."

Casca stepped up to the door, touched his cap respectfully

and took the proferred half-penny for which he was expected
to run all the way back to the cab shelter and send a cab
for the woman that the butler's swell had finished playing
with for the night.

"Special service tonight, guv," Casca chirped as he ran
down the steps to the street. "Got one comin' for the lady
right now."

He stepped into the roadway as the cab he had just left
rounded the corner. He motioned to the driver, indicating
the open door, cockily saluted the butler and resumed his
walk, his empty gut rumbling in delighted anticipation of
the treat in store.

An hour later, fed, warm, and almost dry, Casca was
opening the door to another cab, standing to attention, cap
in hand as a swell stepped out. But no penny dropped into
the cap. The bloated countenance that stalked past Casca
did not so much as glance in his direction.

Casca looked into the cab interior. He instantly reached
through the open door to scoop up the leather pocketbook,
stuffing it into his shirt as he closed the door.

The cabbie had climbed down and was drying off the
horse so that it would not catch cold as the chill wind turned
the sweat to ice on its skin. Casca walked to the corner,
glancing back as he turned into the side street. The door to
the house was just closing.

Casca ran. If a bobby stopped him he would say he was
running to order a cab for a swell. Running was risky, but
he wanted to be well away from this neighborhood before
the first police whistle sounded.

As he ran he searched the fronts of the houses for a spot
where he could hide the pocketbook when he did hear the
whistle for to continue running then would be to invite
disaster. He made it the length of a block and slowed to
turn the corner. The only bobby in sight was almost four
blocks away with his back to him.

Casca walked quickly toward him, maintaining his pace
as the bobby glanced in his direction as Casca reached the

corner. The short whistle was answered from somewhere in the new direction. He turned the corner, and Casca had the length of the street to himself. He ran like the wind.

Casca made the turn toward St. John's Wood Station. He went into the tea room, sat down and ordered tea and a bun. Then he went to the men's room and under the gas lamp examined the contents of the pocketbook.

There was a gold sovereign and a pound note, a ten-shilling note, some visiting cards that read: CAPTAIN ROBERT GORDON MENZIES, BARRISTER, with an address in the colonial city of Melbourne, Australia.

Regretfully Casca flushed the expensive pigskin and the cards down into the Thames. He wrapped the sovereign in the pound note and hid it amongst his ragged underwear. Back at his table he ordered corned beef and cabbage and a beer. He wanted to change the ten-shilling note, and didn't wish to attract attention by doing so for a penny or ha'penny. Besides, he couldn't remember the last time he had tasted either beef or beer—or, for that matter, cabbage.

An assistant station master, uniformed like an Hungarian brigadier, or perhaps a Bulgarian lance corporal, came past the tea room calling the imminent departure of the morning express for Bewofsdel.

The name rang a happy chime in Casca's long memory. Best damned campaign I ever was in, he recalled. The Roman legions had chased the wily Britons into the distant mountains, the Romans getting close to exhaustion as they tried to find somebody to fight, the Britons tirelessly retreating and leaving behind their blue-eyed women and strong beer to slow the Roman advance. By far the most effective retreat tactic Casca had ever encountered.

When the worn-out Romans at last called off the chase and returned to their fortified posts, the Britons came out of the hills of Wales, reclaimed their wives and daughters, disdaining to notice that their bellies were swollen with beer and babes. And a little later the Britons cheerfully celebrated the births of a whole new generation of short, crinkly-haired

children, almost indistinguishable from the Calabrians of
southern Italy where Hadrian had raised most of his legions.

Now, he had a destination, a train leaving, money in his
pocket, and the danger of the police who might appear at
any moment. He ate quickly, then hurried to buy a third
class ticket and boarded the train just as it left the station.

CHAPTER TWO

The shouted name of the station roused Casaca reluctantly from dreams of beef and beer and Briton maids. He tumbled out onto the platform just as the train blew its whistle to depart.

Outside the station he looked around at the depressing, ugly, dirty little town. A grimy soot had applied a gray film to everything in sight. Narrow-fronted little houses straggled up a winding road to a giant wheel that turned slowly at the pithead of a coal mine. A single cable turned around the wheel, and Casca guessed that this was the mechanism that lowered miners into the pit.

Of the quaint Briton village of his memory there was no trace. Perhaps the distant green hills were the same.

In the cafe where he breakfasted he learned that the mine was hiring workers due to a recent cave-in which had killed and injured scores of men.

It was work for which Casca had little taste, but it was work. More than once he had been a slave in a mine, so perhaps working in one as a free man might not be so bad.

He quickly found himself a room in the house of a widow and presented himself at the pithead at the start of the next shift.

He was shocked to find that he had to rent his tools and even his lamp from the mine company. They expected him to pay this rent in advance but agreed to take it out of his first pay as they were in urgent need of labor.

The descent was terrifying.

The pit cage dropped unrestrained on the single cable, and Casca felt his balls and his stomach leap upward. Then he almost crashed to the floor as the brake was applied, slowing the cage before setting it down on the bottom of the shaft. A tenth-of-a-second miscalculation by the brakeman, Casca realized, would slam the cage into the bottom at full speed. And the brakeman was at the surface, half a mile above, and operating entirely by guesswork and experience.

The miners immediately set off at a trot and Casca ran to catch up. They were running down a dark, sloping tunnel, all the men shambling, head down, shoulders stooped like apes as they trotted on the crossties of the tramway.

There was no light as the miners had to pay for their oil. Casca struck his head hard on an overhead beam and quickly stooped to bring his height down to the level of the other miners.

They ran for half an hour without slackening their pace, except where subsidence had brought down the tunnel roof to an even lower level. And even at those places that it seemed they knew or sensed like bats, they scarcely slowed, bending their knees to shuffle forward in a squatting position. They also jumped aside from time to time to make way for the skips full of coal being hauled by tiny young girls yoked to the tramway cars by a headband. This child labor had recently been made illegal, but here the pit owners maintained the practice since replacing the little girls with pit ponies would necessitate raising all the tunnel subsidences that the girls were able to wriggle beneath.

By the time they arrived at the coalface, Casca was on the brink of exhaustion. Naked except for his shorts, he was lathered with sweat, panting the hot air in painful gasps. His calves, the backs of his thighs, and the muscles of his back seemed to be on fire.

All around him men were lighting their lamps and getting down on their knees in front of the coal. The face of the coal seam rose only three feet above the floor, and the miners were quickly at work on it with their picks. They were not paid for the time it took to ride down in the cage or for the long run to the coalface. It was almost half an hour since Casca considered he had started work, and so far he was still behind for the tool rent.

He dropped to his knees and set to with a will. The coal was surprisingly hard, and a considerable effort was needed to force the pick to penetrate far enough to be able to lever off a chunk of the black stone.

When Casca felt that his aching arms could not wield another stroke, he paused and looked around him. The other miners were hard at it, working at a methodical rhythm, each stroke adding to their piles of coal. Casca realized with a start that theirs were already much larger than his.

He paused a moment longer to study these small Welshmen, any two of whom he could have easily lifted in one arm. In the dim lantern light he could see that their bodies rippled with well toned muscle, but for all that they were the merest lightweights.

Casca set to again, determined to increase his tally to match that of his workmates. Knowing that overexertion would tire him quickly, he set himself just to match his neighbor stroke for stroke, counting on his extra size to win the extra coal needed for him to catch up.

But when he paused to rest again, he saw that, in fact, his blows were less effectual than those of the small Britons, and that the Welshmen's piles of coal were almost double his. Nor had any of the other miners even paused for so much as a second.

Casca flailed his pick at the coalface, tearing out great pieces of the black stuff, digging like one demented until his arms were trembling with exertion, and his breath was rasping in his dry throat.

He would pay, he knew, for this overexertion when the work ceased and the overstrained muscles tautened against the damage he had inflicted on them.

But he had caught up. His pile of coal was now a fair

match for any of the others. He smiled grimly to himself
as he realized that in this one small matter the curse of the
Jewish prophet worked for him. Tonight the tortured muscles
would give him hell, but by morning the curse that had kept
him alive for two thousand years would have worked to
repair all the damaged tissue, and his body would perform
tomorrow as if it had worked at a coalface for twenty years.

He had just recommenced digging when he stopped; he
didn't know why.

All along the face the other miners had stopped too. They
all crouched expectantly, pick in hand, as if listening for
something.

They all heard it in the same instant. Their picks dropped
to the floor, and the miners scurried on all fours out of their
workspace, then got to their feet and ran.

Casca was with them. He had felt, rather than heard, the
tiny sound just as he had first heard it in the copper mines
of Aegea more than a thousand years before. The earth
above them had shifted.

Another sound followed, louder, an ominous, crunching
noise. And then a thunderous crash as the ceiling of the
tunnel fell in behind them.

They retreated farther along the tunnel and waited. A few
more pebbles fell here and there, and then there was silence.

Cautiously they returned to where the tunnel was blocked
by fallen rubble. They began to pick at it with their bare
hands, clearing the way to their buried tools.

A foreman arrived, alerted by the noise and the sudden
draft of air that the fall had pushed before it. Behind him
came a team of timberers carrying stout beams which they
quickly rigged into position to support the ceiling. Another
team arrived with shovels, and the clearing of the fallen
material went faster.

The fall had been a small one, and within an hour Casca
and his workmates were again kneeling before the coal seam.

And now they worked even faster. The fall had cost them
an hour's coal-winning. There was no pay for idle time.

While the timbering team worked, Casca had reflected on his circumstances and concluded that he was scarcely any better off as an employee in this English coal mine than he once had been as a slave in an Aegean copper mine.

To be sure, there were no chains, and the British miners did not go in fear of the whip. But in these cramped mine tunnels there was no room to wield one, especially at the coalface where a slave master would have had to kneel alongside the miners.

Besides, Casca had experienced both ends of the whip, and he knew its limits. Neither men nor animals could be whipped to work beyond their capacity without provoking either collapse or rebellion.

It was sheer economic necessity that drove these British miners harder than any whip-hand could hope to do. The mine owner could increase that pressure whenever he wished by charging more rent for the tools or for the miners' cottages. And by increasing the storekeepers' rents, the mine company could even increase the cost of the miners' food and clothing.

At the end of the day Casca was as weary as he could ever remember being in his life. From force of habit the men ran from their work as they had run to it. The ascent in the cage was not as bad as the descent had been. The cage rose slowly, hauled up by a steam winch at the pithead.

On the surface the miners quickly dispersed to their homes where the only real meal of their day awaited them. Most miners avoided eating before they started work and had a single sandwich at the coalface for lunch.

Casca found himself alone. And worse, feeling lonely. At times like these the curse of the Nazarene hurt him deeply. For him there was no wife waiting in a cramped cottage to help him out of his pit gear, to wash the coal grime from his body, and set a steaming bowl of soup before him. No kids playing on the floor before the cheery coal fire in the stove.

Not tonight nor any other night. More often than not it

suited Casca to be wifeless and childless, but this bleak little village in the lowlands of Wales was not adapted to the needs of single men.

He made his way to the room he had rented. It occupied the back corner of the widow's house and had to be entered from outside like the privy that was next to it. It was cheap because this village was full of widows with rooms to rent. The inevitable accidents in the mine saw to it that there was never a shortage of widows.

To his surprise, his landlady had a tin bath full of steaming hot water waiting for him in his room with soap and a scrub brush.

Casca read in her eyes the mirror of his own loneliness, and through her shyness he saw clearly that she would be happy to scrub his back for him. Or to do anything else for him that he wanted just to be able to feel once more that she was a woman and could play her part in the life of a man.

Casca enjoyed his bath and the boiled mutton that the widow served him in her kitchen. But he evaded the invitation in her eyes, patted the two tiny, fatherless children on the head, and left for the pub.

The Miners' Arms was tiny, too, barely big enough for the half dozen men and dogs who were in it when he arrived.

Casca's life settled into a routine of the day's hard work, hot bath, supper, a few beers, and a game of darts, then home to bed so he'd be ready for the same the next day. Only Sundays differed.

CHAPTER THREE

One Sunday—he hardly knew what made him do it and blamed it on the first summer weather—he invited his landlady and her children to spend the day with him at the beach.

The hour-long ride in the train was the first time ever outside the village for the children, and the beach was an undreamed of experience for Gwyneth.

They walked the length of the pier and ate ices while they watched a Punch and Judy show. The children paddled in the shallows, shrieking whenever they splashed themselves. Casca stood with Gwyneth on the pebbles of the beach and watched and thought of other beaches with golden sands and golden-skinned, naked women.

He took the little family to a restaurant and treated them all to fish and chips and persuaded Gwyneth to join him in a glass of bitter.

That night he went to bed as usual but was awakened after a few minutes by a knock at his door. Wrapping himself in a towel, he opened it to the outside darkness, but by the starlight he could just see Gwyneth wearing a nightdress. She walked into the room and over to his bed. "Do close that door and come to bed," she said matter-of-factly. And as he joined her she added, "I'm not going to make a habit of this, and I don't expect you to marry me, but I need a man, and I think maybe you could use a woman."

Casca didn't argue. She never did mention marriage again, but she came to sleep in his bed every night.

Casca's routine was very much improved. By day he

admired the cheerful fatalism of his workmates, and by night he enjoyed their company over darts and beer and politics.

Hugh Edwards, a straw-headed giant, was one of his favorites. The big Welshman had educated himself by countless nights in the Mechanics' Institute Library and was an entertaining source of invective in the cause of Welsh nationalism.

Hugh wanted a free Welsh state with its own parliament, taxes, and customs. He also argued that Wales should have its own army but was agreeable to it being always available to British command in time of war.

He also insisted that Wales should have its own king. "There's plenty of the old noble blood," Edwards insisted. "We don't need to import inbred German princelings. We'll have a Welshman for King of Wales—the first true Briton to sit on an English throne since Henry the Eighth."

Casca ordered a pint of bitter and smiled into it as he remembered the mixture of Italian blood that the Romans had contributed to the Briton strain. He was sipping at it slowly when he heard a cheerful voice at his ear. A widely grinning face appeared behind another pint pot at the other side of the table.

"Wot'cha cock? Down the mine ain't cha?"

"Yeah." Casca looked at the Cockney stranger.

"Me too. Saw yer in the cage when I was signin' on at the pit 'ed this mornin'. Me first day down a mine. Bleedin' 'orrible ain't it?"

"It sure is," Casca smiled.

"Dave's the name," the Cockney went on. "Dave Prince, but I ain't Welsh. Straight Lunnoner. You're not from here either?"

"I sure am not, mate. I'm an American. My name's Rufus Casterton. Friends call me Cass." He appraised the lightly built Cockney. "You a miner?"

"No way, mate. Jes bein' down there's enough fer me. I'm a tally clerk. Heaviest thing I lift is me pencil—and still it's the worst job I've ever had—or even heard of—in me life. But it is a job, and there ain't none in Lunnon.

"Shouldn't be here, really," he went on, "drinkin' money I ain't really got. But me landlady made it plain she fancies me. She's a mine widder—the mine company allows her to keep renting her cottage so long as she takes in single mine company workers like me. She's nice enough, but blimey, I don' want to get settled in this burg. Nor would I want to knock 'er up and shoot through on 'er. She's got two brats already from her miner."

Casca found that he was nodding in agreement.

"The mines is tough enough on men," Dave said, "but they're bloody 'ell for women. Town's full of widder women."

"There were nearly some more today."

"So I 'eard. Were you in that lot?"

"Yeah. Don't know what happened. Some sort of gas explosion and then a fire. We all got clear—this time."

"Yeah, well," Dave's voice was suddenly quiet and serious, "that 'ole is a damned dangerous place. A man'll be safer at the war."

"War? What war?"

"You 'aven't 'eard? The Serbs done in an archduke, and Austria and Serbia are goin' to war over it. The Germans want to be in it too, and Russia will likely back the Serbs."

Another man spoke up from a corner. "And the French and the Russians are allies so the frogs will be in it too."

"Well," said another, "the German Kaiser Wilhelm is our King George's cousin, so I suppose we'll be with Germany against the frogs and the Russkis."

"Good thing too," came from another miner. "Time we taught the frogs another lesson. They've been getting real uppity in Morocco."

"But we supported them when they seized Morocco."

"Yeah, but we had to, to keep Germany out."

"Well, it's time we bloodied the Czar's nose anyway. He's blocked us in Persia, in Afghanistan, and in Tibet, and all of them are rightly British.''

"No," a miner with a newspaper asserted positively, "it says here that we're a party to that Russian alliance with the French, so we'll be with them against the Germans.''

"What?'' "Are you crazy?'' "Us fight alongside frogs?'' The shouts came from all over the room. "Us with the Russians—impossible!'' "Didn't we just close the Dardanelles to keep the Russians out of the Mediterranean?'' "The Russians want Afghanistan so they can push us out of India—how can we side with 'em in Europe?'' "How can we side with France?'' "They're confronting us in Africa and in Egypt.''

The conversation became a babble of shouts, and Casca borrowed the newspaper and sat among the arguing miners to read it.

The dateline was June 28, 1914. In Serbia the Premier, Pašić, had discovered a plot by his head of military intelligence, Colonel Dimitrević, who had set up a secret society called Union or Death with the avowed aim of creating a pan-Serb nation and liberating all Serbs from the yoke of the Austro-Hungarian Empire. Pašić alerted the Austrian Emperor, Franz Josef, in a message so cautiously worded that it could not be understood and so was ignored. Austria sent the Archduke Ferdinand to visit Bosnia which Austria had annexed in 1908, on a tour of military inspections, and at Sarajevo a Bosnian Serb, one Gavrilo Princip, had shot the plump Archduke and his wife, the Duchess of Hohenberg.

Serbia? Casca pondered. Who would go to war over Serbia? Or over an archduke. Must be a rumor. Aloud he asked: "Who is this archduke anyway?''

"Nobody knows. Europe's full of archdukes, I believe. Some sort of cousin or nephew of the Austrian Emperor— and of the old Queen of course.''

Well, for sure, Casca thought, there can't be a war over that. He put the matter out of mind and offered to buy the likeable Cockney a drink.

CHAPTER FOUR

Over the next few days Casca's view of the European situation became more and more confused. Austria seemed to be reconciled to the loss of its archduke, and Premier Pašić's warning to Austria had cleared Serbia of any guilt. The assassin was in prison awaiting trial, and both the Serbian nation and the leaders of Bosnia's Serbian population had expressed their regrets, and it seemed Austria would accept. The matter seemed to be at an end.

But Germany—it was not clear why—was determined to become involved and, for no discernible reason, was threatening to invade France although neither the French nation nor a single Frenchman had inolved in the assassination.

The lowlands of Belgium provided a level pathway from Germany to France with highways, railroads, and canals all leading directly into northern France. So Germany delivered a formal ultimatum demanding free passage for its armies. It was a demand no country could possibly accept.

The nation of Belgium, a recent British invention, had only come into existence in 1831, and was neutral. So now the potential conflict had widened to include the British Empire, and through the Triple Entente Treaty, Britain would be allied with her long-term enemies, Russia and France.

Casca's daily toil in the mine had become easier as his muscular body had adapted to the demands made upon it. He came to tolerate the heavy, dangerous work and more

and more enjoyed the company of the tough, little men he
worked with. Gwyneth made no demands on him, except
in bed, and his life had settled into a routine that was not
at all unpleasant, especially when compared to sleeping out
on the London embankment and running to open cab doors
in the hope of a penny.

Each evening he came back from the pit to a hot bath
and a fine hot meal, then off to the pub for a few beers with
Cockney Dave whose landlady had similarly moved in with
him. Over pints of bitter Casca and Dave would discuss
their undesired, but irresistible, marital arrangements, the
worsening economic conditions of the mine workers, and
the increasingly bizarre politics of Europe.

On August fourth, its ultimatum unanswered, Germany
moved on Belgium, and sixty thousand German troops
crossed the frontier, swamping the twenty-five thousand
Belgian defenders. The German spearhead attacked Liege,
the key to the narrow pass to the Belgian plain.

England and France immediately declared war on Germany, Austria, and Hungary. Russia quickly declared that
she too was at war, joining England and France.

The declaration of war gave the two reluctant spouses
just what they needed. They bade farewell to their landladies
and their underpaid jobs and headed for London to join the
volunteer force being raised by Secretary of War, Lord
Kitchener.

Half a million men flocked to the colors, almost half of
them miners. Conservatives, liberals, the Labour Party, even
the Irish members, supported the war and the recruiting
campaign. First Lord of the Admiralty Winston Churchill
was to direct the war, personally supervising strategy. Sir
John French was to command the troops in the field and
was ready for a short, decisive campaign that would wrap
up the whole affair before Christmas.

The recruits were paraded through the London streets in
their civilian clothes, mostly worn-out and none too clean,

Crowds cheered them, women threw flowers, and old men clapped them on the back as they passed.

"Popular war," Cockney Dave smiled.

"They all are—when they start," Casca grunted, unimpressed by the crowd's patriotism.

As they came to Whitechapel, they were saluted by a bobby sergeant. Hugh Edwards shook his fist at him in return. "I know that bleedin' perisher," he snarled. "Three months ago I was marchin' with the unemployed, and the bobbies broke up the march. That swine tried to break my 'ead with 'is baton—and now he salutes me."

A pretty woman in a white dress and a flowered hat ran to pin a flower on Dave's chest and kissed him on the cheek. Dave grinned happily then chuckled to Casca, "And a week ago she'd have stepped into the gutter to avoid me."

Casca and the other ragged men within earshot laughed with him. The army of the rear had become the army of the front.

But Lord Kitchener was only accepting the cream of young British manhood, and two thirds of the recruits were rejected as chronically undernourished or otherwise medically unfit. Many recruits were barely eighteen, and many, having lied about their ages, were younger.

Cockney Dave passed fit, his youth making him acceptable, and Hugh Edwards and Casca were readily enlisted for their physiques, but several of their friends were summarily rejected by the army doctors.

The doctor who examined Casca was intrigued by his numerous scars but accepted his explanation that he had survived a number of mine accidents. There was scarcely a miner who didn't carry some scars. But when he looked into Casca's eyes, the doctor was puzzled, then began to feel uncomfortable. There was something in the eyes that was older than the face. A thousand disappointments had made these eyes as unfathomable as a mountain lake.

The first recruits were drafted into the Territorials, the

expeditionary force formed in 1910 as an elite, amphibious
corps intended to be always ready for immediate overseas
service.

For Casca, the Territorials were something of a surprise.
The 125,000 professionals were still clad in the khaki uniforms that had been designed for the South African war
against the Boers in the previous century. Only a handful
of veterans from that war had seen any action. The rest
were proficient in musketry, but their commanders seemed
to have little understanding of the handling of troops other
than enforcing crushing discipline.

Chief disciplinarian was the regimental sergeant major,
a strutting martinet in a shiny, peaked cap with a voice
rarely heard at any pitch below an angry scream.

Reveille sounded at six, and RSM Norman's screech tore
through the barracks hut.

"Orright, orright, orright. Come on, you lot, let's 'ave
you out 'ere then."

Norman's raucous voice called the roll, men stepping one
pace forward in response to their names. Until he bellowed,
"Atkins, Thomas," at which a dozen or so men stepped
out, Casca and Cockney Dave among them.

"I thought your name was Prince," Casca muttered to
Dave.

"It ain't that neither," the Cockney answered, "but I
saw Atkins on the form and thought, well, that'll do."

"Damn," Casca muttered, realizing that he had made a
mistake. He too had liked the look of the sample name on
the form in the recruiting booth and had thought it would
serve as well as any.

RSM Norman didn't seem to think the number of Atkinses
strange; indeed, he was bellowing for more. "Come on,
come on, you 'orrible lot. I've got about twenty more Atkins,
Thomases on this list, and I want 'em all out here!"

A few more men stepped forward reluctantly.

"What's the matter with you lot? Don't you know your
own names?"

It turned out that numerous recruits had adopted the same name from the sample form for their own reasons as had Dave and Casca. Many more, unable to read at all, as almost all Englishmen were illiterate, had simply copied everything—name, age, marital status, number of dependents. About a fifth of the recruits had been enlisted under the name Thomas Atkins.

In a rare moment of wisdom, RSM Norman decided to accept the situation and leave it to the pay corps to sort out. By the time the confused roll call was over, all the recruits were laughingly calling each other Tommy.

Norman's cretinous monologue continued through a three-mile run with an unending tirade of threats and sneers.

At seven there was a merciful break for breakfast, but by seven-thirty the unmerciful shriek was snarling its dissatisfaction with the cleaning of the spotless barracks. And at eight RSM Norman's snarling dominance really began with the drill that occupied most of the rest of the day.

The repetition of the simple routines bored and exasperated Casca. Hour after hour, day after day, they repeated the same basic drill. There was no weapons instruction or any combat training. Their torturer's only interest was in endless marching, and he drilled his charges until their actions lost all semblance to normality, and they moved in a series of timed jerks like so many wooden dolls.

Norman carried a pace stick, two canes fixed to one head and separated at the ground to exactly the size of the regulation pace of the British army.

The regimental sergeant major especially liked to humiliate his immediate subordinates, the drill instructor sergeants, and he would march alongside one of their squads twirling his ridiculous cane and loudly lamenting the tiniest deviation from the sacred length of pace. One of his favorite drill square pastimes was to combine a number of squads and drill them unmercifully, catching them out, tripping them up, and greeting every tiny fault with a long string of abusive sneers partly directed at the recruits and partly at their squad instructors, who squirmed mightily at every taunt.

During one endless sequence of left turn, right turn, about turn, into line, form fours, form column, quick march, Casca found himself in the front rank with Cockney Dave in the rank behind and Hugh Edwards farther back. The sergeant major wheeled them to the left, and Casca saw a chance to turn the game on the tyrant. He had once, and not too long ago, been a drill instructor sergeant in the British Army and thought he could teach Norman a thing or two.

He stepped out mightily, calling softly to Dave and Hugh to stay with him. Their rankmates kept up, and the nine men opened up a wide gap ahead of those in the turn.

"Come on, come on, you 'orrible loafers, you bleedin' bums," Norman shouted at his men, "shake it up, shake it up."

The entire squad stepped out, but the wheel slowed those who were in the turn, and they had to hasten even more as they came through it. The result was that half the large squad was strung out along one side of the drill square, while the rest were jammed into one corner of it.

The furious Norman saw his mistake too late. He turned his attention to the runaway leaders. " 'Orright, you lot in front, slow down will you!"

But Casca had already slowed so that he was now leading a bunch of about thirty recruits, with more catching up at each pace. He now slowed to a crawl. The corner of the square was coming up, and Norman ordered another left wheel. Casca almost marked time through the turn then streaked away again.

Behind him he could hear Norman harassing the stragglers to lengthen their stride—ensuring yet another pile up while Casca strung the whole column out across the next leg of the square.

Norman raced to meet the head of the column and fell into step alongside Casca, twirling his pace stick along the ground beside him. But Casca had anticipated him and was moving at exactly British Army regulation pace. For several seconds RSM Norman was silent as his pea brain strove to understand what was going wrong.

Hugh Edwards, though, was not fooled. "You've done this drill before, haven't you, Cass?" he whispered.

"Some," Casca admitted as RSM Norman returned his attention to calling up the tail end of the lagging column. Casca smiled to himself as he recalled all the times that he had been a rookie on a drill square. The smile widened as he reflected on the times that he had been the drill instructor, a job he had always excelled at.

The sweating NCO brought the column to a halt, dressed ranks, formed them into line, then back into a column. He then marched Casca's rank to the rear, having concluded that somebody in this rank, probably the oversize Casca, had an erratic pace. He then recommenced the march around the square. Within a few minutes he had to call another halt. At the head of the column Dave and Hugh contrived to distort his every order, while at the rear, Casca was working to the same purpose. But to the perturbed RSM, the column seemed to be falling apart by itself.

As the disruption grew worse, more and more of the recruits tuned into the game, and soon the entire column had passed that point at which discipline ceases to be effective. There were simply too many men too determined to fuck up—and Casca had shown them a way to do so without ever actually committing any offence.

Norman ranted and raved, stamped and screamed until he was almost frothing at the mouth. The men's vengeance was complete when a major, riding past on a splendid horse, was so appalled at the display that he rode over to the drill square and summoned the RSM.

Norman handed over the recruits to one of his sergeants who promptly called the men to order. They responded readily and correctly. He reformed them into squads, then handed them over to their squad sergeants. In a few minutes the drill square was in regular order while the sorely discomfited RSM stammered an explanation to the major.

Casca was gratified but not impressed. A Roman officer would have taken over himself. Even emperors such as Trajan and the great Julius were apt to themselves undertake the instruction of soldiers, challenging them in strength and dexterity. Casca had once so matched swords with Hadrian who took great pride in his skill as an instructor and frequently seized the opportunity to try out his men in the line. Hadrian was a master swordsman, and Casca a mere trooper, but he had acquited himself well, as Hadrian had expected.

That night the recruits gloated over their victory. The morning, however, brought the raucous voice and vicious snarl back into their lives with redoubled malevolence. But when it came to drill time, Norman left them to their D.I. sergeants.

When eventually they came to combat training, Casca was appalled at the elementary level of sophistication. What passed for unarmed combat was no more than a simple set of armlocks which almost required an opponent's cooperation to be effective.

Weapons instruction was an even greater shock. Each company was issued one Lee Enfield .303 rifle with bayonet and an empty five-round magazine—for the instructor. The recruits were issued plywood dummies and had to pretend to manipulate these in a parody of the sergeant's motions with the one real rifle.

Casca recalled his first training in Domitian's legions. The Latin word for army was derived from the word for exercise, and early and late Roman recruits were instructed to march, run, jump, swim, carry each other, handle every type of arms that could possibly be utilized for offense or defense, for work in a distant engagement, or for close combat. They moved always to the sound of flutes playing the Pyrrhic martial dance. And all their training arms were double the weights of those they would actually use in battle. Casca felt something close to despair as he hefted the six-ounce replica of a nine-pound rifle and looked around him at the callow boys with whom he was about to go to war.

Replicas were also used to introduce them to the Mills bomb, an explosive grenade with a time-delay fuse that commenced when a lever was released as it left the thrower's hand, the lever being normally held in place by a pin. The practice dummies merely looked like the real thing, lacked both moving lever and pin and were absurdly light.

The only worthwhile training was in the use of the bayonet. The Territorials were expert musketeers, and since their day-of-fire issue was only twenty-five rounds per man, the bayonet was as important as the bullets. Day after day they practiced at the straw dummies that represented German soliders, taking turns to use the few real rifles.

"In! Out! On guard!" the instructor bellowed, and the sweating soldiers would stick their bayonets the regulation four inches into the dummy, withdraw them, and return to the on-guard position.

They also practiced against each other. Two men faced each other with real rifles and bayonets and went through the motions of trying to stab each other. They learned how to thrust and how to feint, how to wrestle down the opponent's guard, and how to turn their rifle so that the opponent's own force brought his weapon down, uselessly out of the way and with his body off balance.

Casca was impressed but shocked to find that this represented almost the whole of their combat training. Bullets were too scarce to waste on target practice, and each man's total marksmanship training consisted of firing one five-round magazine.

The worst shock of all was the pay. In the mines Casca had earned enough for his simple needs with always something left over to treat Gwyneth and the children. He now learned that his army pay would be less than half that, and he had already signed an allotment form remitting what turned out to be most of it to Gwyneth on the first of each month.

"I don't believe it," Cockney Dave lamented. He too

had signed over what he had thought was half his pay to
his ex-landlady.

When he had fought in Britain for the Roman Emperor
Domitian, Casca had been paid a piece of gold per month,
about twenty English pounds a year. And at the end of
twenty years, he would be paid off with three thousand
denarii, about two hundred pounds sterling. After twenty
years a British soldier would get about a quarter of that.

"Well," Cockney Dave ruminated, "for all that, it beats
being down the mine."

CHAPTER FIVE

The troopship was yet another shock. It was a derelict hulk laid up ready for scrap and had now been pressed into urgent military service. The British Army, despite its global responsibilities, had no regular means of conveying its troops abroad and depended on commercial shipping companies.

The SS *Plymouth* was an antique rust bucket, a tramp steamer registered in Panama, barely seaworthy, commanded by an elderly neurotic with a polyglot crew hastily recruited from numerous waterfront bars. One hold had been converted to convey the troops with crude timber bunks one atop the other and hammocks slung between. The only ventilation when the hatch covers were closed was a single pipe vent.

The troops spent most of their time in endless lines waiting for their food, drinking water, to use a toilet, to shave, and to wash. The hold stank like a cess pit, but the soldiers were forbidden to travel on deck.

The Territorials disembarked in France on August fifteenth, the day the last Belgian resistance collapsed. The huge German army had entered Liège on August fifth, but Belgian troops under the determined command of diehard General Leman had demolished all the city's bridges and retreated to a dozen modern, thick-walled forts on high ground.

Over the next ten days, German 420mm siege guns demolished the forts one by one. Colonel of Fusiliers Erich Ludendorff succeeded in getting lost with his three brigades and was harassed severely by civilian snipers. He gave orders for the summary execution of these "Francs Tireurs," and the German firing squads were kept busy shooting every civilian they found at large. Many hundreds were slaughtered including a number of elderly priests.

On August 10, Fort Barchon was captured from the rear, then Ludendorff and his fusiliers got lost again. By August 15, Ludendorff had found his bearings and laid siege to Fort Loncin. Toward nightfall the gallant General Leman was carried unconscious from the ruins.

The previous day, August fourteenth, German troops engaged a large French force in Lorraine. The French general Lanrezac was defeated in what became the ten-day battle of Charleroi.

Meanwhile the British Expeditionary Force of ninety thousand men under the Boer War hero Sir John French was idle. The troops spent their days in unending, trivial drill, digging latrines, cleaning and recleaning their tents, and telling and retelling the numerous rumors.

It seemed that Germany had eighty-seven divisions, each with eighteen thousand men, equipped with Mauser rifles and Maxims, the machine gun invented by an American-born Englishman. Each German division was backed with thirty-six 105mm and sixteen 150mm howitzers.

The French had mustered sixty-two divisions, each with seventeen thousand; barely a million men, about two thirds of Germany's strength. And they had three hundred medium and heavy cannon against Germany's three and a half thousand.

The British Expeditionary Force totalled a mere ninety thousand in six slender infantry divisions armed with rifles and bayonets and five cavalry brigades with lances, sabers and carbines. Their only heavy weapons were four five-inch guns and two machine guns per batallion. There were also a few bicycle detachments, field telegraph and carrier pigeon detachments, and some observation balloon units. When the Kaiser was advised of the arrival of this force, he sneered,

"A contemptible little army."

At last, on August twenty-second, the British troops were issued equipment. Far too much equipment, it seemed to Casca. Each man was weighed down with a total of sixty-six pounds.

Casca divided his mountain of junk into two parts—the rifle, bayonet, ammunition pouches and two Mills bombs he wanted, also the water canteen, entrenching tool and eating equipment. The rest he set aside to dispose of at the first opportunity.

It was an opportunity that he didn't get. They were marched to the town of Mons where the French Fifth Army was locked in a losing struggle with superior German forces. They marched along country roads lined with trees beside fields and farmhouses. The soldiers occupied the center of the road, and both sides were jammed with French refugees, as many heading for the German border as were heading away from it. Most of the groups consisted of a stout farmer in the lead—blond, blue-eyed ones heading north, swarthy ones moving south. Behind the farmer came a high-laden, horse-drawn dray hauling everything of value that could be carried—brass beds, barrels of wine, furniture, perhaps a plow, a butter churn. Behind the dray came numerous children and women, all carrying as much as they were able to bear.

The over-laden British troops arrived on the outskirts of the town as darkness fell and had to set up camp in the open, blundering around by lamplight.

At dawn the next morning they moved into some empty French trenches while their twenty-four pieces of artillery were dragged about and eventually aimed at the German lines.

The hastily set up British guns were too far away, too small, and too few to have any real effect other than to alert the Germans that an attack was imminent.

At eight o'clock, in broad daylight, the Tommies climbed out of the trenches, each man hampered by his enormous pack and accoutrements. Second lieutenants with wire cutters opened narrow passages through the giant sausages of barbed wire, and they stumbled forward into a hail of artillery bombardment accompanied by withering machine gun fire. The tracer rounds from the machine guns made long lines of white light as they reached for the British troops.

Stooped almost double, they ran into the rain of lead.

To Casca's right a Highland division was advancing, led by a group of young boys in kilts playing bagpipes and drums. Behind these boys came the subalterns, only slightly older and armed only with swagger sticks and holstered pistols.

The German trenches were only four hundred yards away, and the intervening ground had been churned up by constant French and German artillery fire for the past ten days so that now it looked like the surface of the moon.

Casca stumbled at the lip of a shell crater and fell into it, rolling down the slope to come to rest in the bottom pinned by his heavy pack. He struggled up and saw that he shared the crater with two corpses, one German, one French, and both stinking. He shrugged his way out of his pack and abandoned it then climbed the far slope of the crater and paused to survey the scene of action.

All around him men were dying, blown to bits by shells, or cut in half by machine gun fire. Second lieutenants with swagger sticks were pacing back and forth exhorting the men to advance. Here and there a few Tommies would clamber out of a crater and run forward to be torn to pieces in the fire storm, and every few moments one or the other of the subalterns would fall.

A lieutenant passed close to Casca's crater, a boy of perhaps eighteen, his muddied pink cheeks streaked with tears, his swagger stick waving urgently as he called for another charge.

Casca, cursing himself for a fool, rose to his feet and ran forward, and a number of other men ran with him. They advanced about ten yards, men falling with every stride until only Casca and the lieutenant were on their feet. And then Casca was alone.

The enemy trenches were only a hundred yards away when Casca fell again. He lay still, staring at the barbed wire entanglement that topped the German trenches. Every few yards along the trench there was a machine gun, and all of them were spitting flame in his direction. Around him British troops were either hugging the ground as he was or screaming out their lives in messes of blood and lead and dirt.

The last of the officers seemed to have died or perhaps had learned enough to keep down. Only the Highlanders over to the right were still advancing in the wake of the bare-legged boy musicians. None of their officers had survived, and they were led by a sergeant.

As Casca watched, the German mortar crews concentrated their fire on this sector, and he saw first the drummers, then the piper, and then a sergeant and most of his following soldiers fall to the ground as the shells burst around them.

The wire was now less than fifty yards away, but it was clear to Casca that they were not going to reach it. Suddenly the boy piper leaped to his feet, his pipes held above his head in one hand. Then he ran for the English lines. Good thinking, Casca decided quickly and took off after him. All along the line Tommies were getting to their feet and fleeing too.

But the carnage continued. The machine guns poured lead after the retreating backs, and more men fell.

Then Casca was at his own wire, searching desperately for an opening while all around him men fell to the machine guns. There were no openings. The wire had been re-entangled as soon as the charging troops were clear of the trenches. And all the wire cutters were out in no-man's-land with the dead subalterns.

Inside the wire stood Regimental Sergeant Major Norman, wire cutters in hand, but he was not about to use them. He paced back and forth, his impeccable boots and cap peak glinting in the sunlight, abusing the troops and screaming at them to turn around and attack the Germans.

Casca succeeded in getting the butt of his rifle beneath a roll of wire, and a number of other men ran to join him, all lifting together until there was just space enough for Casca to wriggle through on his belly.

RSM Norman ran toward him. "You 'orrible, worthless coward! You rotten disgrace to the race! Get back there and fight like a decent English soljer! You no-good . . ."

His voice died in his throat as Casca calmly shot him from where he lay, and the tirade ceased. A moment later Casca had opened the wire and Tommies were pouring through it into the safety of the trench.

Casca leaned against the wall of the trench and worked the action of his .303 to eject the spent cartridge then removed the magazine and squeezed a fresh bullet into place.

"Hope I don't have to shoot too many more Englishmen," he muttered to himself. "I don't like this war already."

He looked out across no-man's-land toward the German trenches. Shaking his head he muttered to himself, "I don't see how men can stand against these machine guns. We could be here for years."

A Major Blandings appeared on the other side of the trench. Purple in the face, he stammered his outrage. "Disgraceful. Running like chickens. Not a man amongst the lot of you. Scarcely a single shot fired."

Casca stared at him calmly, just managing to restrain the desire to shoot him too. The furious officer was still ranting when whistles sounded all up and down the line. The machine guns commenced firing and Casca turned to see a thick wave of Germans rushing for the trench.

He fired deliberately, each bullet accounting for a man. Then he reloaded the five-shot magazine and fired again. Beside him everybody was doing the same, and the chatter of the machine guns was continuous.

The Germans fell in hundreds, but more kept coming.

They were only a hundred yards away when Casca heard the bagpipes and a moment later, a ragged drum beat.

The boy piper and one of his drummers were moving back and forth on the earthworks. The piper was limping, and the drummer's sleeve was red with blood and he occasionally missed the beat, but they played as if in a peacetime parade in London. They marched to the opening in the wire and through it, heading for the oncoming waves of German troops.

Casca didn't want to go, but he found himself swept up in the tide of men who clambered out of the trench and ran into no-man's-land behind the two boys.

From somewhere he heard orders: "Fix bayonets! Charge!" And he found himself obeying, although he had a profound contempt for bayonet fighting while there were bullets available.

The German riflemen could have cut them down, but the wild music from the kilted boys and the long line of threatening steel unnerved some of the men in the front rank, and they faltered. Other men blundered into them, and their charge lost momentum and cohesion.

Then the two forces met. Many of the Germans had emptied their magazines and needed to reload. Their bayonets were still on their belts and they quailed before the Tommies' flashing steel. Even those with bullets ready only had time to fire one round and were still working the bolts of their rifles when the British closed with them.

A lot of Tommies died and a few Germans, but many Germans stopped in their tracks, and not a few turned and ran. Soldiers behind them who could not see what was happening turned and ran too, and the British quickly broke through their lines.

Those Germans who had continued their charge were now at the wire struggling to cut through the entanglements in the teeth of machine gun fire with British bayonets at their rear.

The heavy Lee Enfield rifle was a yard long, and the bayonet another eighteen inches. Together they made a very effective pike, and the professionals who made up the main strength of the British force were well trained in its use. They fell upon the Germans from behind, stabbing them through the kidneys, clubbing them with their rifle butts.

The attack stalled. There was some fierce hand-to-hand fighting, but when it came to steel on steel, the Tommies had the better of it. More and more Germans turned back, and soon the entire force was in retreat.

Casca was glad to see them go, and made no attempt to follow. He was mightily relieved to hear the piper sound the Retreat, and he readily turned to follow him back to the trench.

At their trench Major Blandings was furiously waiting as he upbraided them again. There were also a number of provosts questioning men at random, as it was clear that RSM Norman had not been killed by a German bullet. Norman's replacement was strutting back and forth with a clipboard in his hand, demanding that all soldiers account for their sixty-six–pound packs which were lying all over no-man's-land.

Casca found a quiet angle of the trench and lay down and closed his eyes.

"This is some army I've gotten myself into," he cursed to himself. "They're more concerned about their bloody bookeeping than they are with the fighting. What the hell do they think we're here for?"

A moment later he heard the new RSM shouting at him.

Casca opened his eyes and glanced toward the man and lifted his rifle with one hand so that it pointed as if unintentionally at the RSM's gut. For a long moment the two men stared at each other. Casca's glance was quizzical as if he were awaiting an order to fire. The RSM's eyes were at first furious, then surprised, and finally cautious. He turned away and sought somebody else to harass while Casca again relaxed and closed his eyes.

CHAPTER SIX

But there was to be no rest. The whistles sounded again, the machine guns opened up, and Casca got to his feet to see yet another wave of gray-clad Germans racing toward the trench. They were easy enough to shoot. Casca downed a man with every shot, and the Germans were so closely packed as they ran that even the most ill-aimed shot was sure to hit somebody somewhere.

But there were simply too many of them. Thousands of them. Bagpipes and bayonets would not turn this horde.

Neither would the Vickers machine guns. Each British batallion had only two of the cumbersome, water-cooled, belt-fed weapons, and these were prone to jam if pressed to fire rapidly for any length of time. They were also apt to "hangfire," the cartridge exploding as the breech opened, generally destroying both gun and crew.

Casca had soon used his ammunition issue of twenty-five rounds, and was fast using up the fifty rounds he had stolen. All along the trench men were cursing as they ran out of ammunition. Then one of the machine guns stopped, and a moment later the other fell silent.

Casca looked out into the onrushing swarm of Germans, their Mausers flashing fire. And behind them as far as he could see was wave upon wave of field-gray uniforms and rifles.

"Well," Casca muttered, "Sir John French said this would be a short, brisk campaign. I guess he's right."

He heard and obeyed the order to fix bayonets. Why not?

A useless tactic for a hopeless situation.

The Germans were now cutting their way through the wire, and the Tommies had no choice but to wait for them.

Then he was thrusting his bayonet into a German's calf, then into another one's gut; hot, sticky blood sprayed over him as he withdrew the steel. As they got down into the trenches, the Germans were handicapped by their own numbers. They could not fire for fear of hitting each other, and the defenders' lack of ammunition now mattered much less. The desperate Tommies stabbed and clubbed with their empty rifles. Here and there men lost hold of their weapons and grappled with their bare hands. British officers were using their revolvers to good effect at close range, and the Germans were forced back.

"Fall back!"

Casca sighed when he heard the order and hurried to comply, pausing only long enough to grab the ammunition pouches and magazines of some Tommies who had died before they had used all of their miserly issue.

They raced about five hundred yards to the reserve trench. Casca was relieved to see machine guns being set up and realized that they had not jammed or run out of ammunition but had stopped firing to be readied for this withdrawal.

Behind them in the abandoned trenches sappers were at work frantically placing explosives and detonators and stringing wires. Dead men were being propped up, their empty rifles pointing threateningly toward where the next wave of Germans would come. Medics with red cross armbands were loading shot men onto mules or stretchers, but most of the wounded were left to add their groans and screams to the chorus from no-man's-land.

From behind the trenches Casca heard horses and the squeal of wagon wheels, and shortly cases of ammunition were being passed along the trench. There was a quartermaster sergeant with the inevitable clipboard, and a corporal stood over each crate, but in the rush Casca found it easy to grab over a hundred rounds, and he quickly loaded the spare magazines that he had souvenired from the dead.

The Germans had regrouped and were already leaping into the abandoned trenches. The British sappers set off their charges, and great eruptions of dirt and bits of bodies were blown skyward. The five-inch guns joined in the action and wreaked havoc amongst the confused Germans. But the delay was brief, and in a matter of minutes Casca was again standing to at the lip of the trench squeezing off shots into the advancing mass of Germans.

"Bloody hopeless," he heard an infantryman lament. "It's a simple game of numbers—and they've got 'em. The way it's going, the Jerries will be in Paris for supper."

Casca agreed. They had been rushed to Mons to reinforce the battered and outnumbered French Fifth Army, but their "contemptible little army" with its inadequate firepower was an insignificant contribution. It seemed clear that Casca had once again chosen the wrong side.

The enemy apparently had men to spare and plenty of ammunition that they carried in ten- and twenty-round magazines. It also appeared that they carried their spare ammunition in already loaded magazines so that reloading took only a second, whereas, at best, an adept Tommy needed eight seconds to remove his empty magazine, squeeze in five new rounds, and replace the clip. And Casca mused, Seven seconds is a long time to hold an empty rifle.

The empty trenches impeded the German advance and gave the five-inch guns attractive targets in the milling troops. The sappers had done a good job and were still detonating explosions that killed, confused, and demoralized the attackers. Those who survived pressed on toward the reserve trench but were whittled away by the machine guns and stubborn rifle fire. And where the Germans did succeed in making it into the British trenches, they were always at a disadvantage, unable to shoot because of their own numbers and forced to fight with their bayonets against defenders who outnumbered them in the trench.

The longtime professionals, who made up the greater part

of the Territorials, were very proficient with the bayonet. The British Army, it seemed, still thought of its infantry as pikemen, and they were trained and equipped accordingly.

At sunset the Tommies still held this line, and as darkness fell the Germans withdrew.

Another major appeared, somewhat different from the first. He said his name was Cartwright and congratulated the troops on their splendid resistance. Cartwright told them that he was aware of the ammunition supply problem and assured them that he was working on it. He gave the quite unnecessary warning that there would be an enemy attack at dawn and exhorted them to fight as valiantly again on the morrow as they had during this day.

Best of all, Casca thought, he promoted a number of men to replace the decimated officers and NCOs, elevating the boy piper whose name was George Brotherstone to sergeant. Casca congratulated the new sergeant, and the youth grinned shyly.

"Me mum and the bairns will be glad of the extra pay. And I get to keep the pipes too—there aren't any more boy pipers here. I'm right proud of the old bag." He patted the tartan affectionately. "These pipes were played at Culloden."

Dinner was the usual disgusting mess—chunks of crudely butchered mutton cooked to the consistency of string in a mass of tasteless vegetables, all swimming in a greasy sort of watery soup.

None of the men had blankets—they had made up part of the clumsy packs abandoned early in the battle—so they crowded around the few fires and dozed and yarned through the night.

Casca met up again with Hugh Edwards and Cockney Dave, whom he had not seen since their arrival at Mons. The thinning of the ranks and their successive retreats from trench to trench now brought them together again.

Rumor had it that the German General Kluck had already entered the Belgian capital of Brussels after the Battle of

Tirlement. Most of Lorraine was in German hands, and they were about to take Namur. The French government was preparing to abandon Paris and remove to the safety of Bourdeaux. Austria was about to fall upon Poland. The only good news was that "the Russian steamroller" was underway from the east and would crush the armies of the Central Powers at Tannenberg and then join forces with the Romanians, who had somehow become allies, to save the outnumbered Poles.

Dave was cockily confident and contemptuous of their allies. "It's not as if the Krauts has been up against any real opposition. The show's only just started. When we get some reinforcements, we'll show 'em."

"Some artillery would help," another soldier said.

"Yeah, and some machine guns," said another.

"Just some ammo would be an improvement."

Hugh sat quietly, and Casca, surprised that the big man was not involved in the discussion, joined him.

"What do you think of it, Hugh?"

"I don't rightly know what to think," the Welshman said looking up at him. "When I decided to get into this show, I set out to study a bit about warfare—did you ever hear of von Clausewitz?"

Casca suppressed a smile. "German philosopher, wasn't he?"

"Not quite a philosopher, more of a military thinker. The first thing I read was where he said that no one ever starts a war without first being clear what he wants to achieve and how to go about it."

"Makes sense," Casca nodded.

"Yeah—so what are we doing? Say we beat the Jerries tomorrow—say we win the whole blamed show and push 'em all the way back to Berlin. What then?"

Dave chipped in, "Ah, leave those problems to the generals and the politicians."

"They don't seem to have any more idea of what's going on than we do," Hugh answered. "Look at it this way:

Suppose the Jerries get their way and subdue France. Then what? And what's Russia in it for? And now Romania?''

Dave laughed. ''Don't forget Poland, and they say Italy will be in it soon too. She's treaty partners with Germany and Austria. And maybe Japan is going to fight too.''

''Japan? Japan go to war over an Austrian archduke? Why not China?'' Hugh exploded. ''Why not America? Sweden? Why not bloody Borneo?''

''New Guinea's in it,'' Dave answered laughing.

''Wha-a-at?''

''It's true.'' Casca felt sorry for the earnest miner, striving to understand the inexplicable. ''Australian troops have seized the German colonies, and New Zealanders have taken Samoa.''

''Samoa? Where in the name of God is Samoa?''

''It's a little island somewhere in the South Pacific Ocean. It was a German colony.''

''Where will it end?'' Hugh shook his snowy head. ''What's it all about?''

The expected German artillery bombardment began well before the dawn of August twenty-fourth, but most of the shells fell around the abandoned line of trenches where presumably the guns had been previously aimed. With the approach of daylight the guns started to reach for the reserve trench. There were no direct hits in Casca's sector, but shells fell all around the area so that the troops cowered in the trenches, hands over their ears, praying that the attack would start soon so that the shelling would stop.

They were not kept waiting long. A huge force of Germans skirted the old trenches and mounted a fierce attack on the British position, while an even bigger force moved into the abandoned lines and worked purposefully to turn them to their own use.

Major Cartwright had been as good as his word; he had somehow procured several wagons of ammunition and more machine guns, Maxims, similar to the German guns. The Tommies repulsed the first German attack and left their trenches to chase the retreating Germans. But the Germans retired around their newly prepared trench leaving the British facing fresh troops, well dug in, and with numerous machine guns in place.

The British counter-attack was a disastrous failure and ended with the Tommies being chased back to their trench. Then a new barrage commenced, this time far more accurate, and there were a number of direct hits in the trenches and numerous casualties. When the German infantry attacked again, they overran the trenches, and the British were forced to withdraw to yet another reserve line.

The new trenches had been hastily prepared by French laborers and German prisoners of war. They were un-timbered and in places the sides were already crumbling. The barbed wire was scanty and ill placed; there were no latrines or cookhouses, and the machine gunners were forced to set up their weapons in unprepared and exposed positions. And the sappers didn't have time to do more than plant a few charges in the old trenches, so the Germans were able to occupy them almost in comfort.

All day long the Germans pressed their attack. Only the additional machine guns enabled the hard-pressed Tommies to hold their line.

At nightfall Major Cartwright appeared again, as solicitous and courteous as ever, but clearly worried. He concluded his address with the news that reinforcements and more ammunition were on the way. Casca felt sorry for him as he turned away toward the Highlanders to no doubt repeat his performance word for word.

The food was the same as the previous night, but Cartwright had managed to procure a fresh supply of blankets and a small mountain of firewood. Casca passed the night comfortably enough, but every time he woke he observed the labor crews working by lamplight half a mile to their rear preparing yet another line of trenches for their next inevitable retreat.

August twenty-fifth started the same way as the twenty-

fourth, and ended similarly with the sorely battered British
troops occupying the new trenches which were scarecely
usable, while the Germans had made yet another advance.

Major Cartwright put on a bold front and told them that
there was a relief force at nearby Le Cateau under General
Horace Smith-Dorrien and that his expected attack the next
day would take the pressure off the Territorials. But the
extent of their losses was made clear when the Welsh troops
were merged with the Highlanders. More than half of the
force were casualties. The merger brought Casca under the
young piper sergeant whom he much admired.

Casca woke next to Cockney Dave who stretched and
declaimed, ''The twenty-sixth dawned bright and clear—and
noisy,'' as the first incoming shell exploded somewhere
nearby. Major Cartwright was in the trench talking earnestly
to junior officers. Casca saw that the subalterns' faces grew
more and more grim as the major spoke. Then there were
whistles, bugle calls and George's bagpipes, and, in spite
of the barrage, they were climbing over the top and racing
for the German positions.

''Can't be any worse than sitting here waiting to get hit,''
Dave panted as they ran, and Casca agreed.

It was only half light, and they made it almost halfway
to the German trenches before the defenders' machine guns
started. Behind them their artillery barrage continued to fall
around the now deserted trenches. They were almost through
some of the wire before the surprised Germans realized what
was happening. They were having breakfast, confident that
the British were pinned down by their big guns, not expecting
to go into action for another hour or more.

Casca found that this was the ideal application for the
Mills bomb and regretted that he only had two. Lobbed into
the confines of an enemy trench, the fragmenting grenade
had tremendous effect, killing and wounding several men
and thoroughly demoralizing many more.

The British suffered tremendous casualties, but they did
get into the trenches, and after some desperately savage

close combat, managed to force out some of the Germans.

As the sun came up the situation became more and more confused. Some trenches were securely in British hands, and parts of others were secured. German soldiers were milling about on the open ground behind the trenches without orders from their officers who were rushing from their breakfast in considerable confusion and absorbing numerous casualties as they came within view of the Tommies in their trenches.

Almost half of the German force had been withdrawn to meet the threat from Smith-Dorrien's forces at Le Cateau, and now, for the first time, the Germans found themselves on a surprised defensive and facing troops in somewhat near their own numbers.

Casca saw the officers come running in groups, and he raced toward them. Sergeant George saw him and rushed to follow at the head of a number of his men.

The German officers stopped and drew their Mausers, some of them fitting their wooden holsters to them to convert the pistol to a carbine. So used, with a twenty-round magazine, these were very effective weapons, but the Germans were surprised, confused, and caught it the open. The Tommies cut them down to a man then turned on the approaching sergeants and wreaked similar devestation.

The German Army valued initiative in its ordinary soldiers no more than the British, and all training strove to stifle it. Lacking orders, the infantrymen turned this way and that, firing desultorily and, when they came under concentrated fire from the trenches, taking to their heels.

Sergeant George called to his men to let them go, as the next trench was full of Germans too. But Tommies were pouring out of the first trench, wildly excited at the sight of fleeing Germans and intent on pursuit. George shrugged and abandoned his attempt at restraint and joined in the chase. The leaderless rabble of panic-stricken soldiers was easy meat for the pursuing Tommies firing into their backs. And as more and more men fell, the panic grew. They threw away their rifles and bayonets, ammunition clips, even their helmets—anything they could get rid of that might enable them to run faster.

The Germans waiting in the next trenches were doubly surprised. They were more or less at rest, held in reserve in case they should be needed to reinforce the attack that was not even due to start for another hour. The noise of the action had not startled or worried them. It sounded normal enough as accompaniment to the continuing artillery barrage. But they were mightily surprised to see hundreds of their comrades rushing toward them in wild disarray.

The retreating Germans slowed when they came to the wire, running up and down its length seeking the few gaps left open for the eventual move-up of reinforcements. The delay allowed the Tommies to get even closer, and their rifle fire became even more effective.

Many of the Tommies had emptied their small magazines, and they fixed bayonets and charged the largely unarmed Germans, spearing them through the back or clubbing them over the head with their rifle butts.

From behind the wire the horrified reserve troops watched this butchering. Some turned and ran. Many reached for their unready rifles and strove to get them into action. There was only a handful of officers and NCOs in the area, and their hasty and uncoordinated orders only added to the confusion.

Confusion turned to rout as the despairing wave of terrorized soldiers tumbled into the trenches, overrunning the defenders and spreading their panic to them. Then the Tommies were in the trenches, stabbing and clubbing at the dismayed soldiers while the reserve troops could not bring their weapons to bear for all of their comrades between them and the pursuers.

While many of the British had fixed their bayonets, just as many had paused to reload, and these now opened fire into the trenches from the earthworks.

Within minutes these trenches, too, were empty, the demoralized Germans fleeing wildly to the rear.

Sergeant George, Casca, and some other cool heads called on the Brits to restrain their pursuit. A number of subalterns who had been left behind in the speed and fury of the assault arrived and took charge. Runners were sent back to the main British lines. The captured German machine guns were turned around to face the rear for the inevitable counterattack. Medics arrived and began attending to the wounded.

Cockney Dave led a rush on the German cookhouse, and soon the Tommies were stuffing themselves with good black bread, sausage, and potatoes.

CHAPTER SEVEN

The expected counterattack didn't come. News of the rout of their previously victorious troops came to German HQ just after the news of a forceful and successful attack by General Smith-Dorrien's force at Le Cateau.

At the first news the German commander ordered the reserve contingent from Mons to Le Cateau. His runners arrived at the reserve trenches just as some semblance of order was restored. Company commanders hastened to comply and readied their units to move out for Le Cateau. But before they could start, another runner arrived with orders that they should counterattack the Territorials who had put them to rout.

Then, before this move could be made, fresh orders arrived ordering that the troops stay where they were and wait for further orders. The German general had realized that there was grave danger that Smith-Dorrien would fall upon the rear of the troops at Mons.

Major Cartwright, unaware of the success of Smith-Dorrien at Le Cateau, made a similar mistake and did not press his advantage but waited for the counterattack that he felt must come quickly.

The two forces waited for the rest of the day, only half a mile apart, neither making any attempt to attack the other. Meanwhile, at Le Cateau, Smith-Dorrien's attacking force ran short of ammunition and was unable to gain more ground. The defenders regrouped, and there was another stalemate. But if Major Cartwright made a mistake in not attacking, he made no mistake behind his lines. He pressed into work every laborer and prisoner he could locate. By sunset all three lines of trenches were in good order: large wire entanglements were set up, machine guns were emplaced and well provided with ammunition and water, wounded were removed to the base hospital, and the troops fed and rested. The "contemptible little army" was ready for whatever the dawn might bring.

And what the morning brought was a truly massive artillery barrage followed by a determined infantry assault that cost many lives on both sides but failed to dislodge the Tommies from their positions.

At Le Cateau a similarly determined German offensive tore holes in Smith-Dorrien's lines but did not succeed in overrunning them.

The vicious fighting went on all day with scarcely a pause, and at sunset the positions of the two armies were much the same as they had been the previous evening.

The next day the Germans brought up fresh troops and succeeded in forcing the British back to the next line of trenchworks and that afternoon forced a farther retreat. The following day they forced a withdrawal to the next line and then to the next. And the next day to another that had been readied in the interim north of the Marne River.

The German attacks continued, each with more troops than the last, and the British and French were forced to continually retreat. The withdrawals were orderly, however, and more costly to the attackers than the retiring defenders.

A few days later, the French government did, in fact, abandon the capital and withdraw to Bordeaux, leaving Paris under the control of a military governor, General Gallieni. The Germans had now driven all French forces out of Lorraine and had taken Namur, Longuy, Montmedy, Soissons, Laon, Rheims, and Maubeuge.

On the Eastern Front, the Battle of Tannenberg had resulted in a crushing deafeat for the "Russian steamroller" that had been partly offset by the successful defense of

Poland, inflicting even greater losses on the Austrian forces.

With German forces only fifteen miles from Paris, the military governor saw that the city was gravely threatened and urged General Joffre to mount a general counter-offensive. On September fifth, Joffre attemped to outflank the entrenched Germans, while they made a similar move against the well dug-in French troops and the shrinking British contingent.

The Battle of the Marne raged for five days with neither side able to gain any territory but with enormous casualties on both sides. The French army continued to pour more and more men into action. Eventually, on September ninth, both the army of General Kluck, the conqueror of Belgium, and that of General Bulow fell back; the whole German line withdrew west of Verdun.

Both the French and the British forces hesitated then advanced cautiously. The German line withdrew farther, and the allies made another wary advance. By September thirteenth, the Germans had been pushed back north of the Aisne River where they made a stand.

The allies stayed cautious. The German withdrawal had been orderly, and, it seemed likely, preplanned. They had yielded perhaps five miles of territory but might now be better established in previously prepared defenses. These defenses would surely be hardened with every day that passed.

In the British lines the soldiers argued among themselves, mostly coming down on the side of action. No doubt the same discussions were going on at HQ, but coming down on the side of caution.

An artillery sergeant major appeared and several companies were paraded before him. He addressed them as if they were schoolboys, informing them of some of the intricacies of artillery operations, particularly the need for detailed knowledge of the location of the enemy and of his movements. He said that it had been realized that experienced infantrymen made better observers than artillerymen who rarely saw what they were firing at and so lacked the background for accurate recognition and reportage.

"We need a volunteer," he finally smiled, "for a light-duty job. Nothing too much and right out of the firing line."

Even the rawest recruit could smell a trap. And there were no recruits in the Territorials so raw that they didn't know the first law of military survival—never volunteer.

The sergeant went on, "No fighting involved—the volunteer won't even need to carry his rifle. And he'll get a two-day pass to Paris at the end of his duty."

"What's left of him," Cockney Dave muttered.

"Must be suicidal," Casca replied.

"A decoy duck," another soldier breathed. Not a man in the ranks moved.

"I'd go myself," the sergeant major said in a wheedling tone, and a grim chuckle swept the ranks as each man realized that the danger of being appointed volunteer was getting closer, "but I'm afraid of heights."

Heights? What was he talking about? Casca looked about at the war-blasted landscape of the Marne River Valley. Any heights would certainly be far from this war zone.

The sergeant's tone became more aggressive. "Well then, who's it to be?" he shouted cheerily, clapping his hands together and pacing along the length of the assembled men.

Not even Cockney Dave muttered a witticism. To so much as wiggle a toe might be taken as willingness to undertake the assignment.

"Why doesn't he just volunteer some poor bastard, like always?" Casca mused to himself.

"Come on now, who's for it? Nice ride in a balloon. See the whole ruddy war from a new angle."

A ride in a balloon?

German balloons were over the lines daily, and Casca and his comrades fired at them from time to time. But the large, seemingly stationary, targets proved almost impossible to hit. The balloon was, in fact, always moving. Imperceptibly it drifted from moment to moment toward any point of the compass, up or down, or closer or farther away. And the windage effects at the height of the balloon were quite different from what they were on the ground and impossible to allow for. Casca still tried for one when an opportunity presented itself if he had plenty of ammo to spare, but he no longer expected to succeed in downing one of the huge targets.

Now a ride in one might be something worthwhile. And he certainly had a great desire to see for himself just what was going on in the enemy lines.

He stepped forward smartly.

"Blimey," was Cockey Dave's incredulous gasp. "You, a volunteer? 'ave you gone balmy?"

Within an hour Casca was standing beside a tethered balloon. An artillery captain climbed the ladder to the basket, and Casca followed. He was checking around inside the basket when the captain shouted, "Let go!"

Casca was knocked to the floor of the basket. His first attempt to rise was defeated by the rapid upward movement of the balloon, and he found himself sitting on the floor again. He tried once more, this time hauling himself erect on the side of the basket. He looked over the side.

And promptly wished he hadn't.

The ground was far away, so far away that Casca could scarcely believe it. The deep trenches, the high mounds of earth to their fronts, and the huge barbed-wire entanglements had all been flattened to one level; men inside the trenches disappeared into their shadow. Outside the trenches some tiny creatures moved about slowly and aimlessly like some stupid species of ant. From behind the lines of the trenches came puffs of gray smoke from artillery pieces that looked like children's toys.

Spread out below them was a featureless wasteland. Casca knew well enough that at close quarters no-man's-land was pitted with huge shell craters and strewn with abandoned rifles, steel helmets, packs, clothes, and here and there, arms, legs, a few heads, some whole corpses. But from the

serene height that the balloon had reached, there was nothing
to be seen but a dun-colored expanse of empty land.

Ahead were the German trenches, as indistinct and irrelev-
ant as the British, the same tiny, ant-like figures moving
about in an absurd, unorganized, disconnected fashion. And,
beyond the trenches, some more toy guns emitting puffs of
smoke.

Now and then Casca saw a sort of eruption near or on
top of one of the trenches and guessed that it was a British
shell exploding. But these shells had only the slightest comic
effect on the ants below. A few of them would fall down,
a few others would move a little more quickly for a second
or two, and then it seemed they would all revert to their
previous pointless, slow activity.

"Did you ever see such a stupid, boring, bloody waste
of time in your life?" the officer beside him muttered. Then
a little louder, "Take those glasses and see if you can make
any sense of it, eh, private?" Casca took up the binoculars.
They helped somewhat. He could see that the tiny animals
were indeed men, and looking over the captain's shoulder,
he could now see that the shape of the river below them
approximated the wriggly line on the captain's map. And
some rather straighter lines, he realized, were roads. The
captain was busily dotting the map with new information—
trench and gun positions and troop concentrations. He
pointed to the biggest curve in the river on his map.

"Can you find this place on the ground?" he asked.

That was easy enough even without the glasses. And
when Casca brought the binoculars to bear on the spot, he
saw great numbers of men moving about with field pieces
and wagons.

"Looks like they're setting up a large artillery emplace-
ment," he said.

"Yes. Just as I thought." The captain's finger moved
eastward away from the bow in the river. "And here, somewhere about here—what's going on there?"

Casca moved the glasses slowly, trying to approximate

the line of the officer's finger. He saw a lot of men, many mules and wagons, and some large tents, a few of which were marked with red crosses.

"Looks like a field hospital," he finally answered.

"Oh, I thought it was more guns. Well, we'll leave them alone. Bad enough for the poor blighters being wounded, eh, without being shelled in their beds. But it certainly is a big hospital—must be getting ready for a major push, eh?" He handed Casca a tightly rolled paper on which he had noted the coordinates of what they had observed. "Break out one of those pigeons, will you, and send her off with this info."

Casca reached through the spring door into the pigeons' cage and brought out a bird. Placing the paper in the clip on its leg, he threw it over the side. The bird fell like a stone, but after a little way opened its wings and levelled out to sweep around in a wide circle. Then it headed for the British lines where it knew the bird handler was waiting with some tasty seeds, breadcrumbs, and affectionate pats.

The balloon was now squarely over the German lines, and Casca saw tiny puffs of smoke from the trenches as riflemen chanced their aim at the balloon. But he heard no gunshots or the whine of bullets passing anywhere near.

"Dumb krauts," the officer chuckled. "They don't realize we're moving all over the sky—and even if they could get a good shot, the bullet's losing power every foot it climbs. By the time a round got up here, you could damn near catch it in your hand."

Casca had already caught all the hot lead he ever wished to and had no intention of trying this experiment. But he picked up his Lee Enfield and took careful aim at one of the tiny figures in an open area below. The man seemed to dance away out of the rifle sight, then back in a sort of irregular circle. Casca concentrated and managed to keep returning the tiny figure to the bead of the sight. When he squeezed the trigger he was gratified to see a tiny puff of dirt rise close to the German who turned and ran for the safety of a trench.

"Damn near got him, eh," the captain chuckled. "Curious, eh? We're so big and they're so small, but they make the better targets."

"If I had something like a Mills bomb," Casca answered, "and a way to aim it, I could hit a target down there."

"Yes," the officer pondered, "you're a pretty good marksman. Would you like to go lower and try a closer shot?"

Casca looked over the side at the tiny creatures. They looked so pathetic, their activity so pointless and random. Killing one of them would be like crushing an ant.

"No," he replied, "it's a waste of ammo, and one of them might get lucky and hit us."

The captain nodded and jerked at the line that ran through loops along the tether line, and a moment later Casca felt the balloon start to move back toward the British lines as the Tommies at the aeronaut station hauled them in.

CHAPTER EIGHT

The commanders on both sides remained cautious, the two forces sitting just out of sight of each other, separated by the gently rolling river plains of French farmland.

Casca's company was at breakfast when alarms sounded, and they raced for the trenches. But there were no troops rushing across the enlarged no-man's-land. The threat was in the air.

An enormous dirigible was maneuvering a few hundred yards toward the British lines and perhaps two hundred feet above the ground.

Officers were shouting orders. Men were trying to tilt the machine guns in its direction. Casca and most of the infantrymen were firing their rifles at the gleaming ship. Although it was moving at about the speed of a motor car, perhaps fifty miles an hour, Casca considered that the huge ship made an easy target as it traveled in a straight line and stayed at the same height.

The Zeppelin made a number of passes back and forth and then dropped lower and cruised along directly above the trenches. Explosions erupted beneath it, and fires broke out in the trenches. As it approached Casca could see half a dozen bombs the size of pineapples falling toward his trench, and then he saw a much bigger bomb, the size of a large oil drum.

Every gun was now aimed at the giant airship, and thousands of rounds were being fired at it, the tracer rounds from the machine guns gleaming white in the sunlight. Either they were deflected from the huge metal frame, or they passed harmlessly through the hydrogen bags, but they seemed to have no effect.

The bombs crashed into the trench around the dog-leg where Casca crouched. There was a deafening roar and a great eruption of orange flame. The blast of hot air almost knocked Casca off his feet. Then one of the smaller bombs landed a few yards away, filling the trench with fire. Several men burst into flames where they stood and ran about the trench like screaming torches until they died on their feet. A second large bomb exploded on the ground beyond the trench.

As the ship passed overhead Casca could easily read the name in huge letters on its side: Graf Ferdinand von Zeppelin—L.3.

Casca estimated that the flying ship was at least five hundred feet long. German sailors were firing rifles from the gondola that hung below the balloon and at the rear Casca could see the three huge propellors that pushed the mighty ship through the air.

Somewhere some bullets took effect, probably the heat of a tracer ignited the hydrogen. There was a bright flash. The Germans in the gondola stopped shooting and started to run about in a panic. One of the great propellors stopped turning. The big ship turned sideways in the air and began to slip toward the ground.

It dropped closer and closer to the ground. The nose rose skyward as if it were trying to gain height, but the rear sagged more toward the ground as it passed away from the British trenches and back toward the ridge that concealed the German lines.

But it failed to clear the ridge. The propellors at the sagging rear fouled in the treetops, and the big ship came to a stop. There was a flash of bright flame, followed by a dull crash and then an explosion. Flames darted upward from the propellor area and played around the rigid casing of the balloon.

A great white flash tore the shell apart and a moment

later the sound of an enormous explosion came to the watching Tommies. More flashes were followed by more explosions as one after another the hydrogen-filled compartments exploded.

The fire seemed to have started toward the rear of the gondola where the propellors were jammed in the treetops. Casca could see men leaping from the front of the gondola to the ground, but this part of the ship was still at least a hundred feet high, and none of the men moved after they hit the ground.

The flames spread as dead trees were set afire, and there were still more explosions as successive compartments of hydrogen ignited.

Slowly the nose of the ship came down, the gondola flattening its length among the dead trees. Now scores of men were leaping to the ground and running from the ship. The great rigid gas bag was collapsing over the wreck of the gondola.

Suddenly the whole ship disappeared in a great white flash. The running men burst into flames and fell writhing to the ground, and all around dead trees burst into flame.

Casca stood staring in the dirction of the flames, reflecting that just yesterday he had been flying in a similar, though very much smaller balloon. And as he watched the Germans frying in their tracks, he thought grimly that, no doubt, he would soon be flying in one again.

CHAPTER NINE

Although the British Army had been using hydrogen and hot air balloons for observation purposes since 1884, when they had been introduced into the African campaigns, there was no organized system for utilization of the information that was gathered. Balloon observers identified objectives and passed the relevant map coordinates to gunners by carrier pigeon. The observers also spotted where artillery shells were falling and corrected the gunners' aim with pigeon-carried messages. Artillery officers, however, had little faith in such information and tended to vary it according to information from other sources or through their own intuition.

The difficulties of aerial navigation were considerable, particularly in terrain such as the rolling river valleys of this part of France. There were no dramatically significant landmarks. Farms, roads, rivers, villages, churches were all of similar size, and when viewed from a height were virtually identical.

The speed of a balloon in flight was almost impossible to calculate, so that, once out of sight of their own lines, balloon observers were forced to operate almost entirely by guesswork, although they called it dead reckoning.

Because of these problems, headquarters staff generally discounted or ignored strategic information supplied by the aeronauts on the basis that it could be dangerous to act on information that was of dubious accuracy. But Major Cartwright was convinced of the value of the aerial information and had come up with the idea that it could best be validated by the same observer walking over the ground and confirming or modifying the data.

So shortly after dark Casca found himself in company with six other men crossing no-man's-land, heading for the German lines which were now about five miles distant. Sergeant George was in charge of the party and, for once, was not wearing a kilt but a conventional uniform like the others. All of them were smeared from head to foot in black mud, their faces and hands blackened with soot. Cockney Dave and Hugh Edwards had volunteered to come along, and two more Welsh miners and a Highlander made up the team. For his new responsibilities and in recognition of his service, Casca was promoted to corporal.

There was a fine September moon and their progress was easy enough for the first mile or so. They made their way across the pockmarked landscape skirting shell craters and wading across numerous small streams. They came to the Vesle River at a point where it was crossed by a broad road running east to the city of Rheims. They were still more than a mile from the Aisne River and the troops that Casca had spotted from the air, but there was a large force of Germans on the bridge and, Casca guessed, other detachments patrolling the adjacent area.

Casca had easily persuaded Major Cartwright to open up the armory, and each man was well provided with ammunition and carrying half a dozen Mills bombs. They were also carrying several sticks of dynamite, and Sergeant George readily agreed that the bridge made a tempting target for demolition.

However, whether to take it or not was another matter. Casca was irked by the lack of a specific objective. To blow up the bridge would certainly impede the German advance, and the surprise attack within their own lines would no doubt disturb and demoralize the German troops and confuse their high command. But this war was being run from London, and should Whitehall order a British attack, the destruction of the bridge would severely impede their own offensive.

After much discussion it was decided to plant the explosives while they had the opportunity and to postpone the demolition decision until their return.

Their first objective was to confirm the disposition of the large concentration of enemy troops that Casca had spotted from the air. So it was agreed that no matter what happened, Casca would continue in that direction, alone if necessary. The others split into two groups, Hugh and the two Welshmen to enter the riverbed to the east and work their way upstream to the foundation of the bridge while George and the other two moved beyond the bridge to come downstream to the northern end of the bridge. If either party were spotted, the other would create a diversion and then both would retreat for the British lines while Casca went on to reconnoiter alone.

"It's hardly high strategy," George chuckled, "but it should serve the trick."

The early Autumn weather came to their assistance. The moon clouded over, a chill wind sprang up, and the men on duty on the bridge withdrew to their hut and fire on the north bank.

Both parties made it to the bridge undetected and planted their charges, running a fast-burning fuse up the southern bank. They also lashed Mills bombs to the charges and ran lines from these to the bank. They found Casca in the agreed spot on the far bank and resumed their movement northward toward the Aisne.

They had not gone very far before they heard movement ahead. They guessed a dozen or so Germans on a routine partol and went to the ground in some of the abundant craters until the enemy had passed out of earshot. Sure that they were in safe territory, the Germans were making no attempt at concealment or any real effort to observe. They talked and joked as they moved and would have been easy pickings had not discretion been of much greater import.

The Tommies split up again, this time into three groups: George and the Highlander in the lead, Casca and Cockney Dave following, and Hugh Edwards and the others bringing up the rear.

More German patrols appeared, but they were easily avoided, and the Tommies were soon back together by a small knoll in a bend on the south bank of the Aisne.

Casca spread out a military map and ran over the information he had gathered from the air. Working from the bend in the river, he rattled off the various objectives, describing the field hospital, the artillery positions, trenches, and the places where he had seen the large numbers of men moving field pieces and mule wagons.

Each man took one of the objectives and in turn slipped off into the darkness to confirm its existence. Within an hour they were all back at the knoll except for Cockney Dave who had been told to find the hospital. They waited another half hour, then Casca proposed that he go look for him.

"You can't be spared, Cass," Sergeant George answered in a whisper. "You're the key to all this information."

"But I know exactly where the hospital is. I can find it in minutes—anybody else might be blundering around for hours."

"Aye, I daresay ye can find the hospital, but finding the boy might be another matter. Maybe the Germans have found him. I'm sorry, Cass, but what we've got now is too valuable to lose. I wouldn't risk another man after him if he were me own brother."

Casca couldn't argue. The moon had come out again, and it might well be foolhardy to go looking for a man who might already be a prisoner.

They waited another five minutes, and George had just given the order to move back when Hugh spoke. "There's somebody crossing the river," he said, "a ways upstream. Can I go look?"

Sergeant George agreed reluctantly. "But whatever ye find, come right back."

Hugh slipped quietly away and they waited. In a few minutes Casca heard a movement. He eased back his rifle bolt and closed it gently, the hammer cocked behind the round in the breech. There was a low whistle, and Sergeant George answered. A moment later they heard Hugh's voice, quiet but urgent. "Don't shoot, it's us." And a minute later he and Dave were climbing the knoll.

Dave grinned sheepishly in the moonlight. "Sorry, mates. I've never been out in the country alone before. It ain't like Lunnon, is it? Not a bleedin' gaslight nor a street sign anywhere. And no bobbies to ask the way, either."

Casca had to stifle a laugh.

"Did you find a hospital?" George demanded.

"Oh yeah," the Cockney replied, "that part was easy. It's right where Cass said it would be. Gettin' back 'ere was the part that flummoxed me."

"Let's go get that bridge," George said, and they moved off in three parties as they had come.

Casca was relieved that Sergeant George had decided to destroy the bridge. He endorsed the decision but was even more relieved that he didn't have to make it himself.

"Och, mon," George had laughed at his concern. "It's only a wee bridge. It won't win or lose the war either way. I've seen a bit too much of high strategy to care too much for it. Strategy is the name the high command gives to whatever happens to work—and not too much that comes out of the high command does work. If it don't work, they call it faulty tactics, and blame it on bad decision making in the field. If it turns out that we need the bridge, then it's just too bad. After what I've seen tonight, I sure don't want the Jerries using it against us." He broke into a low chuckle. "And, boy, won't they be surprised when it blows. That makes this whole caper worthwhile."

When they got to the river, it was bathed in bright moonlight. The clouds had blown away, the wind had died, and

now there were a dozen or so German soldiers strolling back
and forth on the bridge. There were more Germans by the
fire on the north bank and, no doubt, more inside the guard
hut and still more patrolling the area. If the decision had
not already been made, Casca would have been for abandon-
ing the attempt, crossing farther downstream, and heading
for home.

As it was, they proceeded according to the set plan.

Casca and Dave moved directly on the bridge, approaching as close to the guard hut as they dared. Then they waited.
In the still night they could hear every footfall on the bridge
and the conversation of the men by the fire.

A sudden explosion around the river bend upstream was
followed by a furious fusillade of rifle fire and then another
explosion.

The Germans on the bridge came running back to the
north bank. Those around the fire lept to their feet and
scurried about for their arms. Another four or five men
stumbled sleepily out of the hut. A sergeant shouted orders,
and most of the men set off at a run in the direction of the
shots. As they reached the bend in the river, a similar eruption
came from downstream. The running men came to a startled
halt. The sergeant who had stayed at the bridge screamed
at them and they ran on. He bellowed at the men around
him, and they ran off in the direction of the new outburst.

Casca and Dave smiled at each other as they pulled the
pins from two Mills bombs. Casca lobbed his toward the
sergeant. Dave bowled his underarm down the slope toward
the shots.

There were two loud detonations and bright orange
flashes, and the sergeant and the fire disappeared.

Casca and Dave charged straight at the bridge. The single
soldier left standing fired at them, but his shot went wide,
and he was still working the bolt of his rifle when Casca's
bayonet opened his gut.

"Messy fucking way to kill," he grumbled as he jerked

the bayonet free, and the German fell into the puddle of his own blood and intestines.

They ran across the bridge and raced along the bank. Casca found the fuses and lit them while Dave was running for the lines to the Mills bombs.

"Forget the grenades," Casca shouted, and the two of them turned and ran up the steep bank.

At the top, they stopped to look back.

Upstream the startled Germans were looking back toward the now deserted bridge while just a few yards beyond them, out of sight around the river bend, George and his two Tommies were splashing across the stream. Downstream another bunch of confused soldiers were also staring at the bridge while Hugh and his mate were rushing into the river.

Casca and Dave opened fire on both groups. The range was rather long, but their fire added to the confusion of the leaderless troops. Both parties ran back toward the bridge. They arrived in time to be blown into the air with the stones and steel.

The Tommies abandoned all caution and ran, whooping and shouting for their own distant lines.

There was no pursuit. They ran until they were out of breath and then huddled in a shell crater to rest. Before dawn they were calling to the sentries in their own lines, and by daybreak headquarters had fully confirmed details of the enemy positions as well as a report on the demolition of the bridge.

CHAPTER TEN

The high command was at last beginning to realize that the war was not likely to be won by sending increasing numbers of infantry into the muzzles of entrenched machine guns.

The original British Expeditionary Force had been decimated, and the few survivors of the ninety thousand elite riflemen were already being referred to as "The Old Contemptibles," a name they accepted with pride.

A new tactic was to be employed, designated "fire and maneuver," whereby brief, high-intensity attacks were to be followed by rapid movement to a different area of the front where the tactic would be repeated. The first trial of this new tactic was to be in the probing of the enemy troop concentration discovered through the balloon reconnaissance and its subsequent confirmation.

One battalion under the irascible Major Blandings was to make the attempt. George Brotherstone was to command the lead platoon and had been promoted to second lieutenant. When Casca congratulated the ex-piper-boy, he laughed bitterly.

"Och, mon, it's not too hard to get promoted here. At the rate we're losing men, some of the cooks will be promoted to general before it's over—they'll be the only ones left with any idea of how the army's supposed to work."

The Scot lowered his voice. "And anyway, this brilliant new tactic is no bloody good—not for these circumstances, anyway. You can bet some smart Johnny thought it up a month ago, and it's taken till now to get it approved. So now they're going to try it whether it's appropriate or not.

"Now that we know where they're strong and where they're not, we should hit 'em full force in the weak spot. If this pussy-footing fails, we'll lose most of the men we have left. And if it succeeds, we'll be inside their lines with not enough men to capture a cookhouse."

Casca had already come to this conclusion himself, and his pessimism increased when he learned that the battalion was being sent directly against one of the strongest German concentrations he had identified. But the high command apparently considered that the enemy could be hurt most where they had the most troops.

Subalterns were supposed to lead infantry charges with a swagger stick, but George wore kilt and sporran and carried his bagpipes. Alongside him marched Harry, the boy drummer who had marched with him into his first action at Mons. As they waited for the order to move out, Casca admired the engraving of George's silver mounted pipes.

"Aye, the black sticks of the devil, the Protestants called them, but they have an honorable history," George said. "The Macpherson of Macpherson played them at Culloden in seventeen 'forty-six. And before that, he played them in the 'forty-five," George chuckled softly. "And, about fifty years before the uprising, an ancestor of mine, one Jamie MacLeish, played them at his own hanging."

"He was a rebel?" Casca asked.

"No," George laughed, "he was a cattle thief."

They left the British lines before dawn and were half a mile into no-man's land when the first of the German artillery opened up on their trenches.

"Aiming to soften us up, like always," Hugh Edwards grunted.

"Aye," said George, "which means there'll be one hell of an infantry attack in an hour or so. We'll likely run into them about the River Vesle.''

"And they'll likely be about ten times our strength,''
said Hugh.

"Aye, you can bet on that,'' George answered. "Nothing
mysterious at all about this war—except to the high command. If we could just get one of those generals out here,
in five minutes he'd learn more about real strategy than they
ever taught him in his five years at Sandhurst Mililtary
College.''

They advanced steadily over the uneven ground and were
approaching the Vesle when the point company got their
first sighting of enemy troops. A large contingent, at least
a battalion, was moving in close order down the long slope
toward the destroyed bridge. But the rolling nature of the
ground hid the river and the ruined bridge from them.

"D'ye think maybe they don't know about the bridge?''
George pondered.

"I'll bet they don't,'' Casca answered. "Maybe somewhere, somebody knows, but these fellas are sure to be
moving on yesterday's orders, just like we usually are.''

"My thinking exactly,'' said Lieutenant George. "And
I'm thinking I might vary my orders a wee bit. 'Fire and
maneuver,' they said. Not so very different from 'maneuver
and fire,' is it?''

Casca laughed in delight at George's ready bending of
the sacred dicta of the high command but felt that he should
warn him against insubordination which was regarded in
the British Army as akin to treason.

"Oh, I ken well enough they'll want my hide if it goes
wrong,'' the young subaltern answered, "but there's nobody
out here with any rank to raise a complaint—and if I fuck
up, I likely won't make it back, so how are they going to
punish me then?'' He pointed up the slope covered with
field-gray uniforms. There were perhaps five thousand men
and hundreds of mules which appeared to be carrying
machine guns and mortars. "We're outnumbered at least
two to one and outgunned maybe ten to one. What are our

chances of winning a confrontation?''

"Not too good," Casca replied.

"Well," George went on, "in a few minutes, they'll be hidden in the dead ground beyond the river, and we could use that time to get across the river. If we can stay out of sight till they get to where they expect to cross the bridge, we should be able to take them in the rear.''

"Good plan," Casca agreed, "but d'you think Major Blandings will buy it?''

"I don't intend to ask him," George answered easily. "I want you to run back to the main body of our troops and lead the major across the stream where we came back last night—beyond the upstream bend. That way he'll be out of sight of the Jerries, and will come up behind them anyway. I'll take the platoon downstream, and we'll have them in a pincers.''

Casca was already moving. An excellent plan, he thought, and too good to risk spoiling through bad timing. He hurried back to where the rest of the battalion was about to move up the slope to the ridge above the river. He gave the ill-tempered major the minimum of information necessary to get him to comply with George's plan.

"Message from Lieutenant Brotherstone, sir. A large enemy force is approaching the demolished bridge and may be unaware of its condition. If you skirt this ridge and cross upstream, the Germans won't know of our presence.''

Major Blandings looked down his long nose at Casca. "My orders, Corporal, are to engage the enemy. Taking into account your information, the best way to ensure engagement is still to continue direct to the bridge.''

"Yes, sir.'' Casca desperately racked his brain for something to say that might prevent the major throwing away the lives of most of the battalion. He improvised desperately. "Lieutenant Brotherstone is concerned that when they find that the bridge is out, the Germans will cross upstream and outflank us.''

"Mmm, yes, we must eliminate that possibility.''

He ordered a single platoon to move to where Casca had
suggested and another to the downstream ford, instructing
them to prevent the enemy from crossing at all costs. He
continued to march the rest of the troops directly up the
slope, and Casca had no choice but to go with them. When
they gained the ridge, they could see the German troops
milling about on the far bank, trying to get organized to
cross the river by the ruins of the bridge.

Downstream Casca could see George and his platoon
already across the river but still out of sight of the Germans.
Upstream the detached platoon had reached the riverbank.

Major Blandings positioned his scant weaponry on the
ridge. The battalion had only been provided with two
machine guns but had managed to obtain two more abandoned by retreating French troops. Ammunition, as always,
was in short supply, especially for the 8mm belt-fed Hotchkiss weapons acquired from the French. There were also
two five-inch guns, but men and mules were still struggling
to drag these up the slope.

The Germans had now sighted the British contingent and
were setting up their guns on the opposite bank. Casca could
see at least six 105mm howitzers, one huge 150mm, and
countless machine guns and mortars. The slaughter was
about to commence—and it was clear that few of the British
troops could possibly survive. Casca resolved to try to im-
plement what he could of Lieutenant George's plan.

"Permission to rejoin my platoon, sir?"

"Permission granted, Corporal. My compliments to
Lieutenant Brotherstone."

Casca saluted and hurried away down the back slope,
heading not for George's platoon but for the one that had
been detached to hold the upstream crossing.

As he ran he heard the German guns open fire, and shells
started falling at random about the area. Not for long, he
thought. The Germans would quickly get the range and
concentrate their fire on the exposed British troops, and

then there would be a massacre.

The platoon at the river was under the command of a pink-cheeked second lieutenant. Following the major's orders, he had his men digging in for a determined stand on the south bank. In this position, they would have no part in the battle and once the German force was across the river, would be easily taken from the rear.

There was nothing to do but to lie.

Casca saluted the young lieutenant. "Message from Major Blandings. This platoon is to ford the river and fall upon the enemy's right flank."

The lieutenant nodded. The tactic would be suicidal but made as much sense to him as waiting out of the fight. He quickly ordered his men out, and in a few minutes the entire platoon was wading toward the north bank of the stream. Once ashore, they wheeled right, and as they advanced around the river bend, came upon the German flank. For just a few seconds they had the element of surprise and made good use of it, firing rapidly into the packed Germans whose attention had been entirely to their front.

But then the Germans turned, and their superior Mauser rifles with larger magazines quickly outmatched the firepower of the British battalion. Mercifully all of the German machine guns and mortars had been hauled to the bridge the Germans had expected to cross, and were now concentrated on the Tommies on the opposite slope across the river so that the entire duel on this bank went on with rifles.

The scanty issue of twenty-five rounds per man was quickly used up, and Casca heard the order he dreaded: "Fix bayonets!"

A little more than a hundred bayonets were about to fall upon the flank of a force of five thousand men, all plentifully supplied with ammunition.

Casca recalled the time, nineteen centuries earlier, when he had gone into action for the first time against the huge German barbarians whose wild ferocity had made them almost a match for the legions of Rome.

Disciplined legions of hand-picked Romans, he groaned inwardly, trained to a pitch of physical fitness and martial excellence, well fed, highly paid and rewarded. And brilliantly led. And always the legions of Rome were better armed and organized than any enemy they faced. The Roman soldiers had confronted the Germans in tight ranks, each man's shield interlocked with the next to form a protective wall. And the upstroke of the Roman short sword turned the short stature of the Romans to advantage against the German giants.

Casca's heart sank as he glanced at his British comrades. Short and slightly built, most of them had never enjoyed a decent meal in their lives and certainly not in this army.

"Charge!"

The young subaltern was on his feet, swagger stick in one hand, a six-shot revolver in the other, running directly toward the German troops. Behind him his Tommies ran forward, the morning sun glinting from their steel.

As Casca ran with them, he glanced across the river. From the top of the ridge, the two five-inch guns had at last opened fire, and shells were falling on the densely gathered Germans around the bridge approach. The four machine guns were also taking a toll.

But the German machine gunners were having a field day as the two thousand Tommies charged down the slope directly into the muzzles of the Maxims on the opposite ridge. Then the platoon was closing with the enemy. Casca saw a dozen startled faces, mainly blond, and most of them very large men. Casca picked out the biggest of them and charged directly at him.

Now Casca could see the Germans' faces. They looked surprised but not frightened; more annoyed, like men engaged in serious work disturbed by a bunch of schoolboys. Although detached from their main force, they had the confidence of their numbers. And the generally puny size of the British troops was a poor match for their brawn.

The big German Casca had picked out seemed to sense his challenge. He flicked his bayonet from its sheath and notched it to his rifle.

"Bad mistake, Heine," Casca grunted. "You could have used that second to crank a round into the breech."

The German rushed toward him. Rushed as had a hundred-thousand Germans in two thousand years. The blond giant ran confidently, sure of his casue, sure of his own prowess. His wide, blue eyes gleamed in his pink, smooth-cheeked face.

He made a long thrust for Casca's gut, but Casca swept it aside. The German grunted in surprise as his Mauser met the Lee Enfield's swinging weight, but he recovered swiftly and parried Casca's counterstroke.

For a moment the two stood chest-to-chest, separated by their rifles as they struggled to break through each other's guard.

"Jesus, but this bugger's strong," Casca cursed as he realized that the bigger man had the advantage. Using his extra height for leverage, he was pushing Casca's guard lower and lower.

"This isn't working," Casca thought. "Gotta do something else."

He looked into the German's eyes; they were almost smiling in their triumph. Suddenly the eyes widened and something like fear showed in them. He stared into Casca's eyes as if trying to read something in them.

Casca slackened his resistance against the German's rifle and allowed him to beat down his guard. The move caught the German by surprise, and his face still looked puzzled as the butt of Casca's rifle smashed into his jaw. The Mauser dropped from his hands as Casca's bayonet ripped deep into his gut.

"Too bloody deep," Casca cursed as he felt the bayonet jam, the dying German dragging it with him as he fell to the ground. He stamped his boot down into the soldier's guts as he jerked the rifle back up, and grunted in relief as it came free.

The German gazed up at him, his intestines spilling out of his torn abdomen. His lower jaw hung smashed from its hinges.

But it was his eyes that held Casca. Still they stared into his. The ruined jaw trembled as he tried to speak. His eyes shouted a wordless question.

Blood bubbled from his mouth, and in the gurgle Casca thought he heard: "What are you?"

He jerked his head away from the questioning eyes just in time.

A rifle shot exploded beside his ear, and he turned to see the man who had fired point-blank for his head. The astonished German was working the bolt action of his rifle for another shot as Casca straightened, bringing his bayonet up with all the power of his legs under it.

The blade sliced into the gray uniform just above the belt and penetrated upward into the chest. One of the great arteries was severed, and Casca was covered in the great gouts of blood that spurted forth.

The Eternal Mercenary wrestled the blade free as the German fell and turned to face the next man.

CHAPTER ELEVEN

The battle raged till the sun went down, and only darkness saved the British from annihilation.

Once the battle was joined, the Germans had been unable to use their artillery and had depended upon successive waves of infantry attacks to dislodge the Tommies from their hastily dug defenses.

From the ridge where the German big guns were now set up, the ground ran in a long slope toward the river, and down into some dead ground. So that after crossing this space, the attacking German infantry then had to toil up another short, steep incline before they came to the top of the next slope, the downside of which ended at the river.

The British five-inch guns and machine guns were able to prevent the Germans from securing this second ridge, so that they could not bring their heavy weapons to bear on the Tommies.

Casca expected the worst for the morning. Surely the Germans would suspend their unsuccessful infantry charges and begin at dawn to saturate the British lines with shell fire.

But well before dawn Major Blandings had the troops roused and moved up the first, short slope toward the German lines. They dug in on the peak of the ridge, which gave them command of the short, steep slope, the dead ground, and the lower part of the long, downhill grade from the German lines.

As always ammunition was in short supply, but some

8mm belts had been scrounged from the French, and most of the men had more than the regulation issue of twenty-five rounds. Best of all, the five-inch guns had been resupplied.

As Casca had expected, dawn brought an intensive barrage onto the now empty British trenches. The Tommies crouched in their tiny foxholes on the ridge and made no attempt to move. Their four machine guns stayed silent, and the five-inchers made no attempt to answer the German bombardment.

"Some sensible tactics at last," Casca said.

"Aye," answered Lieutenant George, "but only because Blandings hasn't any orders, so he can work sensibly on his own. And he can see the shape of the ground.

"If HQ knew we were skulkling here, they'd order us up that slope and right into the Jerry guns."

Casca laughed, "Well, there's no way they can know for a while. We're too far from base for an aeronaut observation team to get here—a tether line that long would pull down the balloon."

"Aye," George chuckled, "and it's the same for the Jerries. And, anyway, the wind is in the wrong direction for them. They can't get a balloon anywhere near here."

For this very reason, the German commander was unaware of the complex nature of the ground close to the river, and he again sent his infantry forward.

The artillery barrage ceased, and a long line of gray uniforms appeared on the farther slope. As soon as they commenced to advance, the British five-inch guns opened fire, blasting the entire hillside. There were so many Germans that every high explosive shell that hit the slope caused some casualties. Sometimes a number of shells would explode more or less together creating the impression of a large number of guns, and the German advance would falter, or even retreat.

The machine gunners on the ridge held their fire until the first of the German infantry was on the opposite downhill slope, and then they hosed them with lead.

These Germans were in an impossible position and most of them retreated quickly. But the German commander ordered them back and increased the number of troops.

Again the machine gunners waited until the attackers were concentrated on the opposite slope before they opened fire.

Many of the Germans retreated again, but a large number ran on through the furious hail of lead and down into the bottom of the gulch. They then had to struggle up the steep incline toward the gunners on the ridge, and the machine guns accounted for almost all of them. The few who made it to the ridge were exhausted and no match for the waiting British soldiery.

Despite the heat of the battle, Casca fired carefully, making every bullet count, and most of the Tommies did the same, conserving their scanty ammunition. Expert though they were with the bayonet, none of them wanted to be forced to use it.

As he shot each sweating German, Casca became more and more angry. The blind futility of their attack infuriated him.

"Dumb Kraut," he snarled as he squeezed off a shot that took off a German's helmet together with the top of his head. "Fuck off, Fritz," he shouted as another turned to run back down the slope. Finally, magazine empty, he got to his feet shouting, "Get off this hill, you useless, fucking idiots!"

And suddenly he was out of his hole, racing toward the handful of advancing Germans, the bayonet glinting at the end of his empty rifle.

His rage was contagious, and several men who were out of ammunition ran with him, and a number of them died, but his anger kept him moving until he was amongst the Germans, shooting, stabbing, and clubbing. Casca's bayonet ran red, and he was quickly drenched with blood. All around him Germans were lying in grotesque contortions as they tried to hold onto their spilling intestines.

In a matter of minutes the hill was cleared of Germans, and Casca and the surviving Tommies ran back to their holes.

Now that the British had exposed their position, Casca expected the German commander to call off the infantry and launch another bombardment with his abundant artillery.

Instead, the infantry kept coming.

"Yesterday's orders," George muttered to Casca as the waves of gray uniforms swept down the hill.

"Yeah," Casca agreed, "we're lucky their command structure is as rigid as ours."

"And maybe as misinformed, too," George said. "D'you know, whenever I get a chance to talk to any of our field officers, they don't want to hear what I have to say."

"I believe you," Casca replied, "but I don't understand it."

He recognized that the war had become a struggle in attrition, but even on those terms, neither side's tactics made sense to him. It seemed that the only orders that either high command could think of were simply to charge directly into the enemy guns, as the Germans were now doing. Few of them got close enough to inflict any damage on the British defenders in spite of their scanty protection. And when the sun went down again, the Tommies were still in position.

The day's losses had been relatively light, and there were almost enough mules to carry all the severly wounded back to the hospital. But the armory wagons brought only some .303 ammunition, a few shells for the five-inch guns, and none for the Hotchkiss machine guns.

Casca made himself comfortable in the bottom of his foxhole, ignoring the cold and the continuing noise. But he could not ignore the thoughts that came crowding into his head. His mind seethed in a mutinous rage at the high command officers and their suicidal orders. He had now been fighting for more than a month, and as far as he could see, to no effect. Each day the two forces attacked each other as if they were all blind and stupid, even drunk. And like drunks, it seemed to Casca that they were fighting without any sensible purpose.

As he closed his eyes, he thought that the next day was going to be hell no matter what mistakes the German commander might continue to make.

CHAPTER TWELVE

The morning dawned bright and clear. And noisy as usual.

The German heavy guns were reaching for the Tommies, dug in on the ridge. The abrupt peak in the landscape made a difficult target, and most of the shells fell either short or long. Those that landed anywhere near the ridge, however, had a devastating effect on the poorly sheltered Tommies.

A dispatch runner had carried the news of the battle to headquarters and returned with orders for a frontal attack on the German position on the farther ridge.

"Sheer fucking lunacy," Lieutenant George fumed as he led his men into the doomed action.

Casca could only agree as he followed. They charged down the short slope, many falling now to the artillery shells that were exploding short of the ridge. The artillery fire continued the slaughter as they crossed the gulch, and then they struggled up the long slope toward the well entrenched Germans.

The German machine guns opened fire, raking the hillside with lead and wiping out huge numbers of British soldiers. The numerous craters excavated the previous day by the five-inch guns provided some protection, and Casca gratefully leaped into one and hurried to use his entrenching tool to deepen it.

All over the slope men were going to the ground in the same fashion, while those who didn't died quickly.

But Major Blandings had other ideas. He had received

orders to engage the Germans and was determined to do so. The impossibility of the task and the misguided nature of the uninformed orders did not concern him. He appeared on the slope amongst the troops, an immaculate, erect, khaki-clad figure, slapping his elegant leather leggings with a swagger stick as he exhorted the troops to move up the slope.

Casca cursed to himself as he clambered out of the safety of his crater. The best thing to do, he told himself, would be to shoot the bloody fool and put an end to the useless attack. But it was impossible not to admire the blind bravery of the man and almost impossible not to follow him.

They gained a few yards and went to the ground again. But after only a couple of minutes, the major was moving once more back and forth across the slope, chanting a string of absurdities about service to king and country, the glory of the empire, and more nonsense than Casca had heard on a battlefield in two thousand years. It seemed, though, that personal battle experience had mellowed the ill-tempered officer, and he no longer abused his men, nor did he again mention cowardice.

Then, for some reason that he didn't himself understand, Casca was on his feet leading a small group of men in a headlong charge into the mouth of the German guns.

Most of his men went down, and when he stumbled on the lip of a crater, Casca was pleased to fall into it. He lay in the bottom, his face pressed into the broken earth, gasping for breath and cursed King George, the British Empire, the British army, its officers, and especially Major Blandings.

But before very long, he was back on his feet and once more racing up the slope with men dying alongside him. When they got to within a hundred yards of the German position, the attack faltered to a halt. Any further advance was impossible. Any man who stood erect for a moment was cut apart by the withering maching gun fire. Even the stupidly heroic major was now sheltering in a crater.

And now the Germans brought trench mortars to bear,

small weapons that fired a high explosive shell. These weapons were not high powered and had only a short range, but
with the machine guns keeping everybody in the craters,
the mortars found their targets.

For a moment Casca closed his eyes in despair. Their
position was hopeless. To turn and run back down the long
slope would only invite a machine gun bullet in the back.
And to move forward meant collecting one in the front. But
to stay put meant that sooner or later he would collect a
mortar shell in the crater.

Casca crawled to the lip of his hole and took careful aim
at the closest mortar crew. The .303 Lee Enfield was a
clumsy, heavy rifle, but it was highly accurate. By the time
he had emptied his five-shot magazine, he had killed all
three of the mortar crew.

He reloaded and turned his attention to a machine gun.
He picked off the man pulling the belt and then the loader.
The gun promptly jammed, and when the triggerman moved
to free the belt, Casca shot him in the head.

He reloaded again, fixed his bayonet, and, calling to the
men of his company, climbed out of the crater and charged
for the silent machine gun. A number of men charged with
him. From somewhere nearby he heard the bagpipes and
knew that George, too, was leading a charge.

Major Blandings was quickly on his feet, directing more
men to follow. All along the line Tommies were coming
up out of the ground and running for the German trench.

When he was almost there, Casca lobbed two Mills
bombs, crouched to wait for their explosions, and then raced
forward. There was no wire, and in an instant he was in
the trench. Other Tommies tumbled in behind him, and they
charged left and right along the excavation.

The trench was a mass of milling men, too close-pressed
to shoot, fighting mainly with bayonets. The advantage was
with the British troops who rarely had anything other than
their bayonets and were ready and skilled with them. The

Germans' lightweight Mauser rifles were ineffective for parrying the heavy Lee Enfields, and most of the defenders fell to the British bayonets before they could bring their own blades into the fight.

But the numbers were with the Germans, and they were quickly supported by troops from farther along the trench. The counterattack pushed the Tommies back to where they had entered the trench. More and more British were now arriving, and the close quarters battle became a confused blood bath.

Tommies on the ground above the trench were lobbing Mills bombs, blowing many Germans to bits, but also blasting some of their own men. The British were shooting down into the trench, but many of them were falling to fire from the defenders.

Inside the trench more and more Tommies were dying as the Germans closed on them from both sides. Casca clambered out and crouched on the edge of the trench, to help other Tommies out. Then they were all running wildly back down the slope, to stumble into the nearest shell craters.

Germans came running from the trenches. Many were cut down by British rifle fire, while those that made it to where the Tommies crouched in the craters were outnumbered and few survived.

But more and more Germans made the attempt, and soon the Tommies were racing back for their own lines with the Germans in hot pursuit. At least, Casca thought as he ran, they can't use those fucking machine guns with the Jerries so close after us.

They reached the gulch and raced across it, but as they began to climb the next slope, the pursuing Germans caught up with them. The numbers in the gulch were roughly even, and the fighting was fast and furious.

And eventually, the British were retreating in good order up the next slope, holding off the Germans with cool, steady rifle fire.

As they neared the ridge, Casca was once more cursing Major Blandings for a fool. No troops had been kept in reserve. Even a few fresh men would have had an enormous effect if they were now to enter the fight from the vantage point of the ridge. But there were no such troops. The only men on the ridge were the machine gun crews, the wounded, and a few runners and medics.

As the Tommies gained their foxholes, their machine guns opened up and cut a swath out of the advancing Germans. Major Blandings stood exposed on the ridge, signalling in semaphore to the distant artillery. He had also dispatched a runner to the guns, but it seemed to take forever before the first shells started to fall on the Germans who were now coming down the long slope in large numbers.

The battle became a repetition of the previous day. The German infantry advanced in wave after wave, each successive attack faltering as it neared the bottom of the long slope and ran into the British cannon fire. Most of these attacks came to a halt as the troops commenced the steep climb out of the gulch and were cut to pieces by the machine guns on the ridge above them.

Late in the afternoon the Germans started to gain ground on the short, steep slope as the Hotchkiss machine guns ran out of ammunition. But when the sun set again over the blood-soaked ground, the British still held their precarious perch on the ridge.

The mules arrived to carry away some of the wounded, the exhausted medics doing what they could for those that could not be evacuated. More ammunition arrived, but nowhere near enough it seemed to Casca.

And a colonel appeared on a bay horse, the highest ranking officer Casca had seen since he had first landed in France. The colonel promoted George to captain, as it seemed the blindly heroic Major Blandings had exposed himself to the enemy fire once too often and had died urging his men into one more fruitless effort at the impossible.

There was also a field telegraph unit with an enormous length of copper wire that they had unwound all the way from headquarters. Through this marvellous invention the HQ staff officers would be able to keep in touch with the battle that was certain to erupt at dawn the next day.

CHAPTER THIRTEEN

Casca woke from a nightmare of empty guns and ranting officers to another nightmare of bursting high explosive and screaming men.

It still wanted an hour till daylight, but the German artillery was laying down an immense bombardment, raining high explosive shells along the ridge where the Tommies were dug in, onto the now empty trenches, and reaching for the British heavy guns farther back. Shells were bursting everywhere, from the farthest ridge to the slopes and down into the gulch below the British position.

Most of these shells were going to waste, but it seemed that the Germans had plenty to spare, and those that did land anywhere near the British lines caused extensive casualties.

Captain George summoned Casca and he hurried to the tiny dugout where the boy officer was hunched over a table. The telegraph equipment was set up on an ammunition chest nearby. George unrolled a military map. He pointed to the mile or so of territory between the Vesle River and the Aisne River.

"I'm not too familiar with this map reading business. You've seen all this from the air," he said. "Can ye tell me just where we are and where they are?"

Casca quickly related everything that he had seen from the balloon, pointing out the main features on the map, and reading off their coordinates. The young man showed a ready grasp of the details.

He turned to the nearby telegrapher and dictated a message: "Suffering intensive bombardment on all quarters. Urgently request reinforcements and replenishment of ammunition."

He grinned at Casca. "I know damned well there's no reinforcements and no ammunition, neither."

He had barely finished speaking when the Morse key started sounding an incoming message. The telegrapher wrote letter by letter as he decoded the message: "No reinforcements available. Cannot supply more ammunition. Attack direct north at eight ack emma."

"Great," George grunted. "Attack? With what? Without reinforcements and without ammunition? And what for? Even if we could make a breakthrough, it would be pointless without reinforcements. It's just a bloody sacrifice. We're not going to win this war by committing suicide."

He turned and moved across the trench, his foot tangling in the telegraph wire and jerking the instrument to the floor. Very deliberately his boot came down on the receiver.

"Pitty, I think I've broken it. Can ye fix it?" he asked the telegrapher.

"Yes, sir."

"More pity," George muttered almost under his breath. "Well, we've got to do something, but sure as hell, I'm not going to attack that hill again. D'ye think they'll attack again?" he asked Casca.

"I'm sure they will."

"Me too. And there's more of them every day, and less and less of us."

The bombardment dwindled and ceased. On the distant ridge, a long line of gray uniforms appeared.

George turned to the only other officer, a young second lieutenant a few years older than himself. "Here's what we're going to do, m'boy. We're going to wait here until those Jerries are within arm's reach of us before we fire a shot. I'll give the word. And every time they retreat, we'll stop firing until they come back. We're desperately short of ammunition, and we're going to make every bullet count.''

He turned to a runner: ''My compliments to our gunners. Their orders are to fire at will while the enemy is advancing and to hold their fire when they retreat.''

The distant gray line started to move down the slope, and the five-inch guns opened fire. The gunners were getting better each day, and they moved their aim down the slope as the Germans advanced, taking a continuous and heavy toll. But there seemed to be no end to the Germans, and whenever the line wavered or turned back, a fresh wave of troops would appear behind them, and the attack would move forward again.

The first wave of Germans eventually reached the dead ground at the bottom of the long slope and started across the flat, taking heavy punishment from the British artillery.

Then they were starting up the nearer slope, and the British machine guns opened up. The Germans broke and ran. At the bottom of the slope, they ran full tilt into the next advancing troops and they milled about in confusion while the artillery and machine guns tore them to pieces.

German junior officers and NCOs ran about the confused troops and quickly brought them back into some sort of order. The uphill advance started again. The British artillery fire moved back up the long hill where more Germans were advancing.

Casca waited at the edge of his foxhole, his rifle trained on a German officer. They came closer and closer, men falling to the machine guns.

Suddenly the bagpipes sounded, and every British rifle spoke at once.

Scores of Germans fell, then more, and again more. They were so close and so densely packed behind each other as they struggled up the steep incline that the Tommies could scarcely miss.

Another fierce volley tore through their ranks, and they fled in wild retreat.

Again the fleeing troops ran pell-mell into their own comrades advancing behind them, but this time those in retreat could not be turned, and soon the entire German line was moving back away. But not for long.

Fresh troops under fresh officers emerged from the German trenches, sweeping toward the British positions in long, gray waves. But the shape of the ground prevented the German machine guns from supporting the foot soldiers, while the British machine guns decimated them as soon as they came close.

Captain George seemed to be everywhere, and especially wherever the fighting was fiercest. He moved from one end of the British line to the other, shouting encouragement, bellowing orders, every so often playing a riotous, skirling chorus on his pipes.

The telegrapher managed to repair his damaged instrument, and it chattered away with messages from HQ. George replied each time with the same message, confirming continuous engagement with the enemy, and requesting reinforcements and ammunition.

The sun passed overhead, and still the confrontation continued. There were dead and dying Germans littered all across the landscape, from the distant ridge where they were entrenched to within a few yards of the British-held ridge. But George's defensive tactic was effective, and no German soldier made it into the British lines. Until late in the afternoon when once again the borrowed French machine guns ran out of ammunition, and even the riflemen were begging bullets from each other.

A fiercely determined assault brought some Germans right to the peak of the ridge and, as luck would have it, at a point in the line where many men were running short of ammunition.

Bayonets alone couldn't hold off the attackers, and some of them dislodged Tommies from their foxholes. But Captain George had foreseen this possibility, and he sounded the retreat.

The Tommies needed no second urging and abandoned their position, running back to the line of trenches from which they had launched their first attack. George insisted that they drag with them the Hotchkisses as well as the two functioning machine guns.

In the new lines George repeated the defense tactic, fighting only when he was forced to, when the enemy was too close to do otherwise.

A series of explosions along the ridge killed or wounded most of the victorious Germans and sent the survivors scurrying back toward their own lines. The handful of sappers had been busy mining the ridge for three days. Now, they detonated fresh charges each time there were enough Germans on the ridge to warrant it.

When darkness brought an end to the action, both the British and the Germans occupied the same positions they had three days earlier.

CHAPTER FOURTEEN

Casca got his promised pass. But only because, unexpectedly, the whole of Captain George's force was pulled out of the line, paid, and allowed leave. Almost to a man they headed for Paris.

There was no transport, and they moved on foot. The road ran past several burned-out villages. The slopes of the low hills were a maze of trenches dotted with large shell craters. Every bridge they came to had been destroyed by dynamite or shelling, and most of them had been replaced by new, lightweight structures hastily rigged into place by French army engineers.

The only trees to be seen were blackened, leafless trunks or blasted, charred stumps. They passed the ruins of houses and barns. Where a wall still stood, it was generally riddled with bullet holes.

Everywhere there were shell fragments, unexploded shells, spent cartridge cases, discarded webbing, packs, abandoned rifles and bayonets, bits and pieces of military uniforms, even boots, and parts of broken carts. Strips of bloodied bandages blew about in the light autumn breeze. Stinking corpses of horses and mules were everywhere, and shallow graves of men were identified by rifles standing butt uppermost in the earth, often bearing a blood-stained uniform cap.

They came to a village adjoining an army barracks. As they passed the gates, they swung open and a small procession emerged. A handful of French soldiers carrying rifles were escorting another soldier in handcuffs. Behind them a small donkey was pulling a flat cart carrying a pinewood coffin. A fat priest brought up the rear.

The prisoner was marched to a post where he was tied and blindfolded. The priest whispered a few words in his ear and made the sign of the cross. The lieutenant shouted, "Aim! Fire!" Shots rang out, and the prisoner slumped in his bonds. Then the lieutenant walked to him and fired a single shot into his ear from his revolver.

As the escort passed on their way back to the barracks, Casca asked one of them what the prisoner's offence had been.

"Incitement to mutiny," was the short reply.

After a few miles they came to areas where there had been no fighting. Houses and barns still stood, but they were abandoned and empty. Most of the fields had been stripped of their produce either by the fleeing farmers or by marauding troops.

Another few miles and they came upon some few civilians. Farmers stared suspiciously at them as they passed the fields. Women and children ran to hide.

Then they were on the outskirts of Paris. Well dressed women were everywhere, but the only men to be seen were walking antiques. Every able-bodied Frenchman was at the front. Except, of course, the politicians who had made their escape to Bordeaux, leaving the city in the care of Military Governor, General Joseph Gallieni.

They passed a newsstand, and Casca bought a copy of the Paris *Herald*, the city's English language newspaper, and the only one on the stand, as the French newspaper proprietors and staffs had fled to Bordeaux with the government.

The front page headline read: HUGE BATTLE ON WESTERN FRONT, and carried a report of the Battle of the Aisne, the four days of carnage from which the Tommies had just escaped.

"Och, mon," Captain George said, "I don't need this

sort of news. What else is happening?''

They found a small cafe and sat at a table, sharing out the pages of the paper and reading aloud to each other.

An amazing piece of news was the success of German ''Unterseeboots.'' During the month of September, they had surprised and sunk several British warships. Most amazingly, these attacks were all attributed to only two German submarines, as most of Germany's twenty-seven U-boats were of the older type, not oceangoing and only capable of operating in coastal waters.

In the diplomatic sphere, numerous countries were still debating whether to enter the war and, if so, on which side.

Turkey was reported to be about to enter the war on the side of Germany and Austria. Italy, formally allied with these powers, was reportedly considering joining the Allies instead to open a Southern Front. Russia was appealing to Britain for assistance on the Eastern Front. Bulgaria was about to enter the war and join Germany in an attack on Serbia.

In an editorial the *Herald*'s millionaire owner, James Gordon Bennett, himself an American, campaigned for America to join the conflict. He cited the increasing use of German submarines against merchant shipping of all nations which, he declared, would eventually involve the United States whether or not the government wished it.

In Rumania the Germans had put their chemical skills to military use, infecting the horses of the Rumanian cavalry with the disease of glanders.

And the war had taken to the air. German airplanes had bombed Paris. British aircraft had raided the Zeppelin sheds at Dusseldorf, Köln, and Friedrickshafen.

There were also reports that none of the Tommies believed of the brilliantly effective use of new inventions such as aerial photography, wireless telegraphy, and field telephones.

''I wonder how you disable a wireless telegraph,'' Cockney Dave laughed.

"Oh," Captain George laughed back, "I suppose standing on the transmitter instrument would work reasonably well."

The cafe proprietor kept them well supplied with beer and anis and begged them to stay when they had finished with the paper and got up to leave. Customers were now hard to come by with virtually every man of drinking age at the front. The waitresses added their pleas—they had not seen a real man in weeks.

They were at last leaving the restaurant when they ran into a group of French poilus in their horizon-blue uniforms, just arrived on leave, too. Cockney Dave had consumed several glasses of anis, and he lurched unsteadily, bumping shoulders with one of the Frenchmen who fell to the ground.

His comrades immediately set upon the Tommies, and in a moment the street was a mass of milling uniforms. The numbers were about even, but all the Frenchmen were of about the same size as the small Englishmen. And nobody on the French side had the physique of George, Hugh, or Casca. Nor did any of them have Casca's phenomenal technique, and most of the blue uniforms were soon lying on the cobblestones while the rest were fleeing down the street.

When it was clear that the Tommies had won, the French restaurateur came running from his cafe. "Gentlemen, gentlemen," he implored, "please accept my apologies for the disgraceful behavior of my countrymen. Pray come back to my cafe and refresh yourselves."

Casca studied the obsequiously sweating Frenchman. He was clearly of military age and fit. It must have cost him a small fortune to stay out of the French army.

The Tommies reoccupied the cafe, calling for anis, absinthe, pernod, beer, and wine. The street fight had certainly raised their thirst, and the Frenchman beamed as he ran busily about shouting at his waitresses to hurry their service to France's heroic allies. The French girls were happy to do so, and were soon having their cheeks pinched and their butts patted by the women-starved Englishmen.

The proprietor opened his secret caches of tinned tongue and goose liver. He produced fragrant cheeses and huge sausages of salami. He offered Turkish cigarettes at ridiculously high prices, but the Tommies had pockets full of money and were glad to pay.

Cockney Dave and Casca cut out the two most attractive women who, it turned out, were the cafe owner's wife and daughter. The greedy oaf was too busy counting the money he was making to notice that the two women had disappeared. He only realized what was happening when he went to his living quarters in search of some hidden cigars that he could surely sell at stupendous prices.

As he entered his diningroom, he was horrified to see his wife's white thighs spread apart on the table with Casca standing between them. He jumped on Casca from behind, and got an elbow in the gut and Casca's heel in his balls for his trouble. He fell howling to the floor, and his cries of pain turned to screams of fury as he saw Cockney Dave's buttocks pumping over his daughter's body on the couch.

Both men were too busy and involved at the moment to do anything more about his unwanted presence. He dragged himself to his feet and over to a sideboard where he opened a drawer and grabbed a large knife.

This was the moment Casca had been dreading but waiting for, and he reluctantly withdrew from the wife's plump body, leaving her spread-eagled on the table among the silverware and plates laid for lunch. She lay there moaning, only dimly aware of her husband and not really interested in anything other than her own satisfaction, that had seemed only seconds away.

Casca turned as the man rushed at him, the heavy chef's knife upraised in his right hand. Casca brought up his left arm and circled it, sweeping away the threat. At the same instant his right hand chopped at the fat throat, and the man fell to the floor.

Casca snatched up one of the large white serviettes from

the table and used it to tie the man's hands. He used another
to truss his legs and returned to his interrupted task. The
frustrated moans of the plump wife quickly turned to cries
of pleasure, and the crockery and cutlery jangled as the
table shook with her spasms.

Cockney Dave had similarly satisfied the girl who was
now sobbing that she had been ruined. As the mother came
down from her peak of satisfaction, she added her wails to
those of her daughter.

Casca took another serviette and crammed it into the
screaming woman's mouth. Dave followed his example,
and they then tied the women hand and foot and laid them
on the floor on top of the head of the family.

They then returned to the cafe, finished their drinks, paid
one of the waitresses, and left quickly. Their comrades had
a fair idea of what must have happened and needed no
second urging to leave with them.

They hadn't gone far when they again ran into the poilus
who were returning with reinforcements in the shape of
armed French military provosts. There was nothing to do
but to submit, and they were taken under arrest to a nearby
French barracks where Captain George was locked in one
cell and the rest of them in another.

The cafe proprietor had meanwhile freed himself and
called the gendarmerie who were searching the streets for
two British soldiers described as "of enormous physique
and hideous aspect and heavily armed." They found no
such monsters, and the search was called off.

At dawn the next morning Casca and the others were
carried on a mule-drawn cart to a railroad station where
they were loaded into a cattle truck. Captain George was
conveyed seperately and was placed in a passenger car with
a number of junior French officers. On the platform a band
was playing the Marseilleise to cheer the long train of cattle
wagons crammed with troops, horses, and mules on their
way to the front.

On the opposite platform another band was playing the

Marseilleise to welcome an ambulance train returning from the front loaded with men in muddied, torn uniforms, swathed in blood-soaked bandages. On both platforms fashionably dressed women were handling out little French flags, sprigs of flowers, and tracts from the Bible.

Cockney Dave considered that they had done well. "If we had behaved ourselves like good boys, we would be walking back to the unit—and we'd have missed this fine entertainment," he said as he tried to fondle the front of the dress of a woman handing him a pamphlet.

Back at their lines they were paraded before Major Cartwright who seemed to have some trouble suppressing a grin as he read to them the note of protest that he had received from the office of the Military Governor of Paris.

"Disgraceful events such as this must be speedily and heavily punished if the unity of the great nations of the Triple Entente is not to founder upon the rocks of such barbarism. At this historical juncture, we cannot afford to tolerate such outbreaks of sordid perversion as these drunken louts perpetrated. This sort of behavior by foreign troops will not be tolerated, and any repetition of such behavior by rabble from the other side of the channel will be met with suitably severe treatment by way of jail, the whip, the rope, or the firing squad."

Major Cartwright looked up from the screed and spoke to Casca. "He goes on to outline your offences, which consist of laying in wait to fall upon law-abiding French troops, holding up a restaurant and consuming its wares without payment, and forcing a French citizen to gag his wife and daughter with his own table napkins while you attempted to violate them on his dining table. Is any of this true?"

"Not a word of it," Casca replied easily. "The poilus fell upon us, we paid mightily for what we ate and drank, and we made no such unsuccessful attempt upon his wife and daughter."

"I'm glad to hear it," Major Cartwright said and dismissed them.

Captain George did not get off so easily. Although he had not been accused of being in the fight, he was demoted to lieutenant for "conduct prejudicial to good order and discipline," in that he had spent his leave in the company of enlisted men and NCOs, a serious breach of protocol in the eyes of the British Army.

But not one that concerned George.

"If they're going to bust me for associating with my friends, they can bust me right back to private, and then it will be no offence."

CHAPTER FIFTEEN

The next morning Casca was posted back to the aeronaut station. He was airborne shortly after dawn with Captain Bryce-Roberts. They were greeted with fusillades of rifle fire as they crossed over the German trenches toward the enemy's artillery emplacements.

"Blighters seem determined to get us," the captain said. "Dump some of that ballast, and we'll take her higher."

Casca dropped a full sandbag, counted to three, then let go another and then another, counting each time and noting with satisfaction that, as he had hoped, they fell in a rough line as the balloon rose and the tether line pulled it back over the trenches, attracting another furious burst of rifle fire. On his next count he dropped a Mills bomb and saw it explode on the earthworks in front of the German trench. The rifle fire ceased abruptly.

"Bravo!" Bryce-Roberts cried. "That shut the blighters' yaps. Pity it didn't land in the trench."

"The next one will," Casca promised himself.

"Hello," Bryce-Roberts shouted, "what's with the hospital?"

Casca focussed the glasses on the blazing tents. Tiny figures were moving in all directions, mule-drawn wagons maneuvering to no apparent purpose. Clouds of smoke and dust were appearing here and there among the tents which were collapsing like card houses.

"We're shelling it, sir."

"Hell, that won't do. Get me a pigeon." The officer

wrote furiously, recopying coordinates from his map. He clipped the message to the pigeon and threw it over the side.

"Bloody fools!" Bryce-Roberts fumed. "They've mixed up the coordinates."

"Maybe somebody decided to make the hospital a target," Casca suggested.

"Then they're worse bloody fools yet," Bryce-Roberts snarled. "There's no point in wasting shells on men who are dying anyway. The job is to knock out those bloody guns that are plastering our boys. And anyway, it's not cricket."

Casca had never understood cricket even when he had played the game. He moved the glasses back to the shambles of bleeding mules and men among the ruined tents. "No," he said, "whatever it is, this certainly is not cricket."

They watched in mounting frustration as the carnage beneath them increased, the British artillery plastering the hospital tents over and over while the unhampered German guns were pouring an equally fierce barrage into the British lines.

Bryce-Roberts was fairly dancing in rage. He turned to Casca. "I say, d'you have any more Mills bombs?"

Casca had brought half a dozen, all he could manage to steal from the vigilant quartermaster sergeant.

"D'you think you could do that trick again if I can get in position?"

"I'd sure like to try, sir."

Bryce-Roberts was spilling gas from the balloon and they were sinking fast, the tether line paying out so that they swept toward the German artillery. They passed so low that Casca could see men's faces, and he pulled the pins from two Mills bombs and hurled them downward. The first fell short, but the second exploded on the ground close to a howitzer. The gun crew fell to the ground, either hit or taking cover, but one gun was at least temporarily out of action.

But now they had drifted beyond the guns, and Bryce-Roberts tugged at the communication cord. They began the ride back as the tether line was hauled in.

This time Casca succeeded in dropping all three Mills bombs among the guns but didn't clearly see the results as the balloon was moving faster and faster and was now once more over the trenches. Casca could hear the whine of bullets and knew that the German rifle fire was coming close. He dropped two sandbags on the men below him and emptied his rifle magazine at them.

The German riflemen were now getting their range, and Casca was looking directly into their flashing gun barrels as he traded shots with them.

But Captain Bryce-Roberts stood at the rail of the basket as calmly as if he were on a yacht at Cowes, shooting a sun-sight with his sextant to accurately pinpoint the position of the guns beneath them. Only when he was satisfied that he had correctly established the coordinates did he tug at the communication cord.

But now the balloon started to fall again, and Bryce-Roberts tugged frantically at the communication cord, shouting to Casca, "Drop all ballast! Dump the pigeons, your gun, everything! The blighters put a hole in the bag!"

Casca didn't need to be told twice. The British lines seemed a long way in the distance, and the German trenches horribly close. And, for sure, the Jerries would have a hot welcome waiting for the balloon crew who had directed the fire onto their hospital. He cut loose all of the sandbags and the balloon rose for a moment, then settled again toward the earth. He helped the captain throw over the pigeon cages and map table.

Casca picked up two large knapsacks. "What about these?" he asked.

"Mmm, parachutes. Curious idea—open like an umbrella. Don't really know if they work." He glanced down at the ground. "We're too damned low to try anyway. Throw them over."

Bryce-Roberts unbuckled his holster. "Guns too!" he shouted. But Casca pointed back toward the German lines where dozens of Germans were clambering out of the trenches and running into no-man's-land beneath the fast descending balloon.

"Mmm," muttered Bryce-Roberts and held onto his pistol. He unbuckled his splendid Sam Browne belt. "The pater wore this at Spion Kop," he said regretfully as he threw it over along with his binoculars, cap, water bottle, and whisky flask. "And this," he sighed as he threw over his brass sextant and its teakwood box, "my grandfather used alongside Nelson at Trafalgar."

Casca had jettisoned his pack, bottle, helmet, and everything he could lay hands on but his rifle and ammunition.

They seemed to be only yards above the ground. More and more Germans were joining the chase, and it appeared to Casca that they were getting closer and the balloon getting lower with their every stride.

"Couldn't be more than twenty feet," he heard the captain shout. "No heroics, mind. Forget the bloody balloon. Jump the moment we hit the ground and run like bloody hell. Our boys won't shoot at us, they can see us now."

Casca looked ahead. It still seemed a hell of a long way to the friendly trench with its protecting entanglements of barbed wire. It was then that he recalled throwing over the wire cutters.

The aeronaut station was way behind the line, and they were now so low that Tommies atop the earthworks of the British trenches were tugging at the tether line where it sagged across the trenches, shouting and waving encouragement while other Tommies were firing at the advancing Germans.

"Cut the wire! Cut the wire!" Casca found himself screaming uselessly.

CHAPTER SIXTEEN

The basket hit, bounced high, hit again and dragged to a stop.

Bryce-Roberts and Casca were tumbled in a heap on the floor of the basket and thrashed about like a fish in a dry bucket, trying to extricate themselves from each other, the basket, the sagging bulk of the balloon bag, and the tangle of lines that seemed to be everywhere about them like a net. The Germans were shooting at them, and Casca prayed that the heat of a bullet would not ignite the hydrogen in the balloon.

Then they were out and running, rifle fire behind them. Casca cursed the bayonet slapping against his thigh and the nine pound rifle in his right fist, but he held onto it. He would need both at the wire.

The British trenches were still a hundred yards away. A large knot of Tommies watching them approach, a few kneeling to aim carefully at the leading Germans. Casca took a single glance to the rear. The furious, but now elated, Germans seemed to be gaining on them, firing wildly as they ran. He saw one man go down, but there were dozens still on their feet.

Fifty yards now and Bryce-Roberts was screaming, "The wire! The wire!" Casca wondered that he could spare the breath, and then heard his own voice shouting, too.

Maybe somebody heard them. Casca saw a sergeant start clipping at the inside wire, and he was joined by an officer and then another. At last they realized the problem, and more and more men worked at the entanglement, bending back the barbed strands as the men with the cutters severed them. But it was slow work, and there were three rows of wire.

Twenty yards. Fifteen. He shot a glance at Bryce-Roberts, and their eyes met. "We'll make a stand at the wire!" the officer shouted.

And then they were there. The Tommies had cut through the first entanglement and were now working on the second. Three or four riflemen on their knees were firing at the Germans. All the others were watching like a crowd at a soccer game.

Casca swung around, firing a shot from the hip which brought one of the leading Germans to his knees. He worked the bolt action as he brought the rifle to his shoulder, now taking aim at the tightly packed knot of Germans. From the corner of his eye he could see Bryce-Roberts standing as if at a practice range, methodically aiming and firing his pistol.

From behind the wire more Tommies opened fire, but the Germans kept coming and kept shooting.

Bryce-Roberts stopped to reload, and Casca saw the pistol drop from his hand as a bullet struck his arm. A moment later Casca felt a scorching pain in his thigh, and he fell to the ground. Bryce-Roberts dropped beside him and both of them lay there reloading, and then they were firing again.

Behind the wire the Tommies were, at last, getting organized and were now pouring lead into the crowd of Germans.

But they kept coming. The shelling of their comrades in the hospital had them enraged, and they wanted the aeronauts at all costs.

Bryce-Roberts coughed, ceased firing, and fell flat. At the same instant Casca felt his left side torn open and was quickly drenched in his own blood.

Two out of three of the Germans were now falling to the British fire, but still they kept coming.

Casca's rifle was empty, there was no time to reload.

The closest German was only yards off. He got his bayonet fixed and pushed himself up onto his knees. "Like a Welsh coal miner," he thought as he ran the bayonet up into the first German's balls. The man went backward screaming, leaving the bayonet free, and Casca hammered it into another German's knee.

It was all he could do. A great wave of nausea engulfed him, his eyes clouded, and he collapsed, thrusting feebly with his bayonet at a third German whose rifle butt smashed the gun from Casca's grasp, then thudded against his skull.

Several hands grabbed him. Others picked up Bryce-Roberts. The Germans turned and ran, carrying the two bodies.

The British troops now had an opening in their wire, and they came pouring out, shooting as they ran. The first of them caught up with the Germans and fought them, shooting, stabbing, clubbing with their rifle butts, kicking and punching as they tried to wrest the two bodies from them.

The Germans stopped running and made a determined stand, decimating the front ranks of the Tommies.

More and more men streamed out from the British trenches, one squad with fixed bayonets led by a lieutenant.

The Germans formed a tight cluster around their unconscious captives and traded bullets and bayonet thrust until there was not a man standing.

Casca awoke in the field hospital.

He ached and burned all over. When he lifted his head from the pillow, it felt as if he had slammed it into a wall, and he fell back groaning as his head throbbed as if under a succession of hammer blows. When the pain in his head diminished somewhat, Casca became aware of his other hurts. His right leg seemed to be on fire. His left side felt as if it had been opened with a wood saw. His exploring hand found blood-soaked bandages on both wounds and on his head.

A white-jacketed captain came to the foot of the cot and

looked down at him. "Well, you're certainly a tough 'un,"
he was saying when the front of his jacket exploded open
and he covered Casca with guts and blood, then crashed on
top of him.

Casca registered the explosion that was followed by a succession of others as shell after shell burst in and around the
hospital. Casca could hear men screaming and cursing. He
was dimly aware of hurried movements as rescuers dragged
wounded patients out of the shambles. But nobody came
near him. He lay unable to move, crushed by the corpse of
the doctor.

The bombardment went on and on. Somewhere nearby a
fire started. Casca was aware of flames near the edge of his
field of vision. He could smell burning and then the sickly
stench of burning flesh. He could hear orders being shouted
and men running. The flames died away, but the stink got
worse, so strong that he could distinguish the odor of
scorched flesh from the stench of the stinking mess that
covered him.

The shells kept coming, landing now in some other part
of the hospital as the Germans methodically laid waste the
entire establishment.

The agony in Casca's side became immense. From long
and painful experience, Casca knew what was happening.
The Jewish prophet who had cursed him with his dying
breath was yet again wreaking vengeance upon him, restor-
ing him to life, the tissues of his body repairing and reknitting
to keep him alive. The process was an agonizing reversal
of the wounding, the tissues tormenting nerve endings in
their reconstruction. It was exactly like being shot all over
again but without the anaesthetic effects of either shock of
unconsciousness.

Casca wanted to scream, and maybe he did. In the bedlam
of shouts, groans, explosions, the bellowing of wounded
mules, the despairing shrieks of the reinjured wounded, he
would not have heard, would not have known, his own voice.

Perhaps he lost consciousness, perhaps the hours of suffering simply ran together in his mind. But at last there was an end to the shelling.

It was night. Small sounds came to him. The whimpering of somebody crushed among the wreckage, the snorting of dying horse, distant shouted orders, from somewhere the crackle of flames, and, farther off, rifle and machine gun fire.

Closer he could see the flicker of lamps and candles and hear people moving about. He could hear the sounds of effort, occasional grunts of distaste or disgust as the dead were manhandled out of the ruins of the hospital tents.

The dead doctor's body was lifted off him, and then Casca felt himself being lifted.

"Boy, this one's really rotten," he heard.

Then a weightless sensation, and he was crashing heavily amidst other stinking, mangled bodies.

"Hey Bill," the voice said again, "we've got a mix-up here—this fella has two left legs."

"Oh, then that'll be Williams, Arthur," a laconic Cockney voice replied. "Williams was in my drill squad—was always turning the wrong way. Our sergeant used to say that he had two left legs."

A rough jerk and they were jolted away to the slow clicking of a mule's hooves and the creaking of wagon wheels.

The ride seemed to go on forever. No sound came from any of those around him, and Casca guessed that he was the only one alive in the cart. It only took another instant for him to realize that he was on the wrong side of a burial detail.

Even before his experience on Calvary, Casca had hated burial detail, and always strove to avoid the duty. But seen from this angle, burial detail was a real, stinking horror.

The bodies had been piled with a great deal less care than meat in a butcher's wagon. Some, like the doctor, had been blown apart, others had been killed while undergoing surgery. Many were in several assorted pieces; arms and legs, spare hands, heads, entrails were loose all about the cart.

And all of this meat had the clammy chill of death and the abominable stink of the rot and decay that had already started.

Casca tried to shout, but there was an arm or a leg across his mouth, and others piled above that. He was struggling to breathe and was so weak from pain and loss of blood that he could scarcely make a sound.

The wagon stopped. He heard the mule driver cursing then felt the wagon move again. This time backwards.

A second later he was flying through air and crashed on a heap of tangled bodies. Some of the bodies broke his fall, but he felt all of his wounds reopen and felt the sticky wetness of blood at his side, his leg, and from his head.

He must have lost consciousness for a moment. The next thing he knew was the smell and the taste of earth. He could hear the light rain of dirt falling onto the bodies above him. He was being buried alive.

The Nazarene's words sounded in his ear as they had when he withdrew his spear on Golgotha. "Soldier, you are content with what you are, then that you shall remain until we meet again."

For the eternal mercenary to be buried alive was a double horror—an unending one, for he would stay alive until the crucified Messiah's second coming. The prophet's curse denied him the ease of even the most dreadful death.

With a mighty effort Casca shifted the leg of the corpse lying on top of him. He got his head beneath the dead man's crooked knee. He could breathe, and the earth was not falling into his mouth. But the effort had cost him dearly. He could make no further movement and lay there, hearing the soft fall of the thrown earth, feeling the blood seeping from his wounds.

And then he was waking to light. Somewhere above him the black had turned to gray. And the gray lightened more as he watched. He recalled his arrival in the grave in the dark of night and concluded that the burial detail had only sprinkled the corpses with a layer of earth and would return with daylight to complete the job.

He struggled to move and discovered that his strength had been somewhat restored. The Messiah's curse had repaired some of the torn blood vessels, slowing the flow of blood and rebuilding the damaged cells.

But not enough. He was still as weak as death, and the weight of bodies above him was too much for his tiny strength. So be it. He closed his eyes and willed himself to return to sleep. Perhaps in a little while the repair would take more effect, and then he would try again.

He was awakened by a dull thump which was followed by several more. He realized that more bodies were being thrown into the grave. A lot more bodies.

He heard a voice. "Well, that's the lot, then. Let's fill 'em in and get done with it."

Casca shouted, "I'm alive! I'm alive!"

"Hey," he heard from above the grave, "did you hear something?"

"Yeah," came the reply, "a voice from the grave, Arthur."

"But I'm serious, Bill," the first voice objected, "I heard some sort of muffled shout."

"Yeah, me too," the other replied, "but I've heard it before, Arthur. Some sort of effect from their being dumped, all jumbled up like, or maybe it's their guts rotting. I suppose the gas comes out through the throat, and it sounds like a voice."

Earth started falling.

"But what if one of them is alive?" Arthur's voice demanded.

The rain of earth stopped. "Suppose one of 'em is," was the answer, "what difference does it make? We'd never find him. We'd have to lift every bleedin' corpse out of that stinkin' 'ole and check 'em over. And we don't even know how. The doctors have already said they're all dead; how are you going to know any different, Arthur?''

Earth started falling again.

"And anyhow," Bill's voice went on, "if we did get someone up alive out of that bleedin' hole, they'd shove him back in the line in a minute, and by tomorrow he'd be back here again."

Earth started to fall more quickly.

Casca took a long, slow breath, exhaled slowly, then breathed again. Concentrating the entire energy of his body into the one effort, he stamped down with his legs and thrust upward with his arms.

"Ow, Jesus," he heard a squawk. The fall of earth stopped.

"Yeah, I seen it too, Arthur," the laconic man said. "It happens sometimes. It's just gas escaping. I expect there's a lot of gas in all of them rotting bodies."

Casca made another mighty effort, and this time he succeeded in shifting the corpses directly above him. Between the bodies he could see daylight and blue sky.

"But, what if one is alive?" the worried soldier said.

"You're going to make a lot of extra work for us, Arthur, if you go on like that," the other answered. "Let's get 'em filled in and get away for our tea."

As the earth started falling again Casca repeated the movement, hurling the two corpses apart with his arms and bellowing, "I'm alive! I'm alive!"

"Well," he heard the laconic voice say, "I suppose you could be right, Arthur. But you're making an awful lot of work for us."

With an enormous sigh of relief, Casca lay back in his stinking hole to wait for the two soldiers to get to him.

The army doctor was sorely confused and more than a little put out. "Only superficial wounds anyway," he scowled. "Don't see why you were ever in the hospital in the first place. You've made a damned awful mess of our records.''

"I can't remember coming here, sir," Casca replied. "Maybe I was concussed."

"Or malingering to get out of the line," the doctor fumed and ordered him back to the front.

"Could you tell me anything of my officer's condition? Captain Bryce-Roberts. We were together when we got hit.''

"Bryce-Roberts? He's gone west," the doctor stated. "You were in his balloon? Why, I was on duty when the two of you were brought in. He was dead already, shot full of holes. You weren't much better, bleeding like a stuck pig and scarcely breathing. I can't believe you're the same man."

Casca certainly didn't wish to attract attention to his recuperative powers. He shrugged. "Well, I certainly feel a great deal more lively now, thank you, doctor."

"I'm a captain, Corporal. There are no doctors in the army."

"No, sir, Captain, I'll remember that."

CHAPTER SEVENTEEN

The laconic soldier had been right. The day after he was lifted out of the hole, Casca was back at the aeronaut station with a new officer, Captain Wothering, who told him that instead of a balloon, they would be observing from an airplane.

"Have you flown in an airplane before?"

"No, sir."

"Oh, it's bags of fun, you'll find."

A motorcycle outfit carried them to where a biplane stood bearing red and blue roundels on the wings and a huge Union Jack on the tail.

"Not ours, of course," Wothering said. "It's a Nieuport, on loan from the frogs."

The captain climbed into the rear cockpit and told Casca to turn the propellor. After two turns he shouted, "Contact!" and when Casca tugged at the propellor blade, the engine fired and the propellor disappeared in a whirling blur.

Casca got into the front cockpit, the ground crew dragged the chocks away from the wheel, and they were moving.

Very fast. Much faster than Casca had ever travelled in his long life. Faster than he would have believed possible. The fastest car or train he had ever been in had not moved half as fast.

The ground ahead was a blur flowing toward the nose of the plane. Alongside the airstrip trees raced past like demented giants running from some awful disaster. Something like the disaster toward which they seemed to be heading, Casca thought grimly.

A terrifying upward lurch, and he felt his stomach thud downward in his body. They were up in the air. Another sickening lurch, this time downward. Casca looked over the side, expecting to see that they were crashing back to earth. But the ground was far below them. They were already very much higher than they had been in the balloon, and although they were still climbing, the motion of the plane was up and down, like a boat riding over waves. The ground below them was moving as if it were being unwound from a roll.

The German trenches came up quickly, and behind them their artillery positions, headquarters, and the ruined hospital.

As they passed over the trenches several infantrymen and some machine guns fired at them. Casca heard Wothering laugh at their attempt. Then he asked in a serious tone, "You alright?"

"Alright? Sure."

"Good. I seem to have caught a packet back here."

Caught a packet? What's a packet? Some sort of cold from this enormous altitude? Why the hell don't the English speak English? Casca thought.

Casca's mind was much too occupied with other things: the horrifying height; the state of his stomach; the infernal racket from the engine; his terror that this racket might cease and the damned thing would fall like a stone.

The nose dipped, and Casca saw the ground. Nothing but the ground. The sky had disappeared, and the ground was rushing up toward them.

A sickening lurch and the ground was gone, and he was staring at nothing but sky. Another frightful lurch, and the plane was flying level again.

Wothering's voice came calmly from behind him.

"Jesus," Casca said to himself, "here I am terrified out of my wits, and this character talks like he's at a tea party."

"Sorry about that, old chap. Getting a bit faint back here, I'm afraid. Fell on the jolly old stick."

A bit faint? Don't tell me he's going to pass out on me.

Wothering's voice confirmed Casca's worst fears.

"Can't hold on, I'm afraid. Don't suppose you know how to fly one of these things, do you?"

"Where does the British Army find these guys?" Casca asked himself. He turned in his seat to shout to Wothering, "No, sir, I can't properly drive a car!"

"Oh, it's much easier than driving a car. Don't have to watch the road. No worries about frightening horses."

Wothering suddenly sucked in his breath with a grimace, and Casca realized that the man was in severe pain.

Caught a packet? A packet of lead—and somewhere that hurt.

"Have a feel about in your map pocket, will you?" Wothering said. "Should be a spare stick in there."

Spare stick? This nightmare was getting worse by the second. He felt around and found the stick. Some sort of baton with a thread on one end.

"Stick the jolly thing in that socket sort of thing between your feet and give it a few twists."

Casca homed the stick in its socket and turned it tight.

"Jolly good. Now pull it back—whoops, not too much."

The plane seemed to be standing on its tail. Casca felt that his bowels would have emptied onto his seat, but that they had congealed into a solid ball. He had the stick clutched to his abdomen with both hands. At least it was something to hang onto.

"Let's ease it forward a bit—whoa, easy now."

Casca lifted up out of the seat. He felt as if the plane were going to throw him out of the cockpit. And now he was looking at the ground again through the faint blur of the whirring propeller. He clutched the stick to him once more.

The ground disappeared again, the sky came back, and

Casca was being rammed down into his seat by some immense force.

"That's the idea. You're getting the hang of it nicely. Now try to keep it about in the middle."

Getting the hang of it? Oh shit, I'm flying this thing! His mind had at last made the connection between the movements of the stick and the swoops and dives of the plane.

He pushed the stick forward. Oh, Jesus, the ground again. Back. Oh, my God! The ground and the sky alternated a few times, and then he had the stick centered and the plane was flying level.

"Hang on, old chap." Casca's grip on the stick relaxed a little, and he could feel the slight pressure of Wothering's hand through the controls.

"Now ease it over to the left, like this—easy."

The lower left wing dropped out of sight, and the ground was moving past below the upper wing. He felt Wothering easing the stick back and moved with him, watching in wonder as the ground vanished, and the wings returned to level.

"Now this way, to the right, that's it."

Then it wasn't too bad, and he could actually feel the vibration of the wings against his hand.

"Now try the jolly old foot pedals. Stick left and left rudder pedal, that's it."

Casca felt Wothering move the pedals under his feet and the plane banked abruptly to the left. Casca closed his eyes, took a deep breath and forced himself to look again. The plane seemed to be pivoted on its wing tips, the ground spinning around below them. Men the size of ants were pointing toy guns at them that fired little bursts of light and puffs of smoke.

They repeated the maneuver to the right, and Casca was almost beginning to enjoy himself.

"By Jove, you've got it nicely. Now try that jigger by your right hand."

Casca took the short lever in his hand and felt Wothering move it gently back, then hard forward. The engine note changed, and Casca swayed forward as the plane slowed and was then pressed back into the seat as it speeded up again.

"That's about all there is to it, old fella. I'm going to take my stick out now. Mustn't fall on it, y'know. You'd never be able to move it."

Suddenly the plane, freed of Wothering's hand, was lurching all over the sky. Everything Casca did seemed to be too much. The plane climbed and dived, banked and swerved.

Gradually the wild movements modified, and they were more or less level.

"Pretty good, old boy. Don't get the nose too high, though. Musn't stall while we're up here. But the trick is to put her down. Ease off on the throttle, bring up the nose, and the bird'll do the rest herself . . ."

The voice trailed off.

"Captain," Casca called with no answer. "Captain Wothering! Captain!" He shouted louder and louder. There was no answer.

Gingerly, holding the stick warily centered, Casca turned in his seat. Wothering was slumped forward, his leather helmet against the control panel.

Near panic. What did he mean about putting her down? He looked over the side at the ground. Surely he doesn't expect me to land this thing?

"Captain Wothering! Captain! Oh, shee-it!"

CHAPTER EIGHTEEN

Casca's stomach rebounded in his belly as he looked down over the side of the plane. Apart from the rocking-horse sensation, the plane seemed to be stationary. And seen from their height, the ground below no longer appeared to be moving.

The river valley ran in all directions as far as he could see, almost featureless. He could just make out the shapes of low hills and what he guessed were roads and rivers. But there was nothing that looked familiar. Or rather, it all looked vaguely familiar and similar in every direction.

The lines of the trenches and behind them the artillery emplacements, headquarters, and hospital were all now out of sight.

Casca was flying as an artillery spotter which simply meant an extra pair of eyes to enable the pilot to concentrate on his flying. His only task was to call the pilot's attention to any activity or features on the ground which the pilot would then record on his maps.

But the maps were in the pilot's cockpit, and there was no way Casca could get to them. Perhaps, he thought, if he were to fly back toward where he thought he might find the German position, he could recognize some minor feature in the landscape that would point him toward his own lines and the small airstrip.

"Never flown in a plane before, eh?" Wothering had said to him as he climbed into the plane. "It's bags of fun, you'll find."

119

"Well, this is no fucking fun at all," Casca fumed. "I don't know where I am. And I don't know where I'm going. I seem to be alright while I'm up here, but I don't know where I can put her down or how to do it. And I can't see the fucking ground except when I'm heading for it."

As he stared desperately around, another horrible idea occurred to him. "I'll bet I'm about to run out of fucking gas."

So what to do? Circle or grid pattern. Circling he could see the ground between the wings without losing too much height.

Out or in?

Out, he decided and pulled the stick left, applying the left rudder as the now unconscious pilot had shown him. The plane dipped into a sharp, corkscrew dive, the spiralling valley rushing up fast.

Oh, great wings of Mercury, how do I get out of this?

Some instinct warned him that jerking the stick back to center and equalizing the rudder would not do. He guessed that such a maneuver would probably break the frail airplane apart.

He gently eased off on the left rudder pedal, coaxing the stick back toward the center. The plane levelled out, but he had lost most of his altitude. The ground now seemed threateningly close. Carefully he inched the stick back right and sighed in relief as the plane soared gently upward and away to the right. He caught a glimpse of the ground but could make nothing of it.

The plane continued to climb in a broad, clockwise sweep, and Casca could now watch the ground at his leisure, looking back and down between the right wings.

But he was none the wiser. The pleasant ever-upward spiral brought more and more territory under his gaze but also removed it so far below that he could not discern anything.

This could be fun—if I knew what I was doing, he thought.

The climb was becoming intoxicating. "I am Icarus," Casca exulted.

Up above, white clouds about the size of cathedrals or maybe cities wandered slowly toward them, passed overhead, and drifted away astern. A wispy gray cloud, much lower than the others, appeared dead ahead of them, and suddenly they were in it. The world disappeared in a gray mist, and Casca felt rain whipping at his face.

Then they were free of it, but still Casca couldn't see, his goggles wet and misted. He took them from his face and was astonished at the force of the wind on his eyes and hurriedly replaced the eye gear.

"Hey, Captain," he shouted over his shoulder, "wake up! You don't know what you're missing!" Casca was quite unaware that a large part of his ecstasy was due to the lack of oxygen being fed to his brain.

The engine was starting to suffer from the same problem, but its coughings and splutterings scarcely registered in Casca's euphoria, and when it cut out completely, he was mightily pleased at the splendid silence. He lay back comfortably in his seat, the clear, sunlit blue sky his own private universe.

"Never," he said to himself, "have I realized just how truly beautiful is the blue sky and these lovely clouds."

Deprived of the lift of its motor, the plane fell out of its spiral and dipped toward the ground.

"Interesting," Casca mumbled, observing that he was now looking once more through the propellor. He also dimly noticed that the propellor was moving much more slowly, so that he could see the circling blades which seemed to be vibrating ominously.

"Shit!" he shouted, "the fucking thing is going to fall off! Well, what the fuck? Don't need it anymore anyway."

He leaned back confortably, streched both legs out against the pedals, and folded his arms over the stick. The plane straightened out, its splendid aerodynamic design allowing it to glide gently on the currents of the mobile air.

Casca was jerked back into wakefulness by the sudden refiring of the motor as their descent once more brought them into oxygen-rich air. He stretched luxuriously like a man waking from pleasant dreams. As if still in dreamland, he blinked upward at the all-encompassing sky. He shrugged himself more erect in the seat and gazed serenely through the propeller at the distant horizon where the land met the sky.

As his lungs filled with richer quantities of oxygen, vague memories stirred of takeoff, some sort of disturbance from the ground, some sort of problem—"Shit!"

Suddenly Casca was wide awake—and sweating.

He tried to stand up in the cockpit to get some better idea of what was going on. And quickly wished he didn't know. The ground was horribly far away, and at the same time, terrifyingly close. And getting closer every moment.

The plane was almost on the ground, much too low to use the parachute that he was sitting on, even if he knew how. Nor was there any way to get his officer out of the rear cockpit.

The plane was flying straight and level but progressively lowering toward the floor of the valley. Unless Casca did something drastic—and what could he do?—they were going to be on the ground in another few seconds. The ground was rushing past at a terrifying speed, much, much faster than Casca's brief experience with motorcars had ever provided.

Lower and lower the biplane dropped until Casca could see individual stones amongst short grass. Goats were running in all directions, bucking and butting at the air in their panic.

Now the ground was alongside him. The plane was still airborne, but the wheels were almost on the ground.

"Ease off on the throttle," Wothering had said, "bring up the nose, and the bird'll do the rest herself."

There was a bump, the plane rebounding into the air.

Another bump. And another bounce into the air.

Casca eased back a little farther on the stick, and closed the throttle more.

He felt the wing stall and the plane settled and trundled along the ground as Casca shut off the throttle.

They rolled to a standstill, but Casca still sat in the cockpit, luxuriating in his new experience—and in his relief to be back on the ground in one piece.

A wave of exultation swept through him, and he climbed out of the cockpit onto the wing. His shout to the captain died in his throat. Wothering had slumped out of sight.

Casca lifted him by the armpits. This provoked a flow of blood which at least reassured Casca that the pilot was alive. He got Wothering out of the plane and laid him on the grass. A bullet had torn through one buttock, missing all vital parts, but the large wound had bled profusely.

As Casca finished dressing the wound and rolled the pilot onto his back, his eyes flickered open. He half sat up, saw the plane, then sank back to the ground.

"Ah, got her down, eh? Stout fella," Wothering said as he lapsed back into unconsciousness.

Casca sat beside the unconscious officer and dismally surveyed their situation.

Almost certainly they were about out of gas. They had two canteens of water, and Wothering had a Webley .38 and maybe two dozen rounds. Casca had been told that as observer, he needed no arms, but had obstinately brought along what he had, his Lee Enfield .303 rifle and its bayonet. He also had all the ammunition he had been issued, twenty-five rounds, and another fifty he had managed to steal as well as a few Mills bombs.

"Why do you give us guns if you don't want us to fire bullets?" he had testily demanded of the miserly quartermaster sergeant major.

"Yer rifle is ter carry yer bayonet," the QSM had snarled, "which is all any decent British soljer should require."

Casca climbed onto the wing and retrieved from the pilot's

cockpit the blood-soaked map. He spread it on the grass beside Wothering. He noted the position of the British lines, the airstrip they had taken off from, the lines of the Germans who had fired at them. None of the information was what Casca wanted to see. Never, in almost two thousand years of poring over military maps, had he ever found what he wanted to see.

"I know where the airfield is, where the British are, where the Germans are." He drew a deep breath and wailed to the heavens the same question he had asked so often over the centuries: "But where the fuck are we?"

CHAPTER NINETEEN

To Casca's great relief, Captain Wothering came around. He tried to sit up, winced mightily as his weight pressed on his mangled buttock, and rolled onto his belly.

"Ah, that's better. I say, old fella, you're a splendid medic. Damned good pilot, too. Where the fuck are we by the way?"

Casca gestured to the map. "Can't pick out a local feature, sir. All I can see is goats and grass. I'm sure there's a farmhouse full of terrified frogs somewhere over one of these little hills. Maybe some kraut troops too. But even a farm wouldn't help. There are farms dotted all over the map."

"Aha, yes, usual problem. Well, we do know some things. For one it's a good bet we're down behind their lines. And if we're not, then we've nothing to worry about." He pointed one slim finger at a mark he had made. "This is where that Jerry machine gun nest is, the one that hit us. Do you know where that is from here?"

"I'm afraid not, sir. I blacked out, and I banked and turned so much, I really have no idea . . ."

"No matter," the officer airily dismissed the problem. "Let's see then. I bought it at just about eleven-fifty ack emma, and it's now twelve-ten pip emma. How long have we been down d'you think?"

"Maybe ten minutes."

"Excellent. Then you were flying for ten minutes. Did you circle?"

"Yes, a couple of times. Quite a bit altogether. But I think I flew straight for some time, too."

"Capital!" Wothering accepted the confusing information as the best available. "Let's say we were doing a hundred and twenty to make it easy. Ten minutes. Twenty miles, right? So the Jerries are something like, say, fifteen miles away in some direction or other. That's not so bad." He shook his head. "Not so good, either, means we've got to survey something like six hundred square miles. Wonder if we have enough gas. Well, let's get at it. We've got quite a few rivers and roads. Must be able to identify something."

He pushed himself up off the ground—and promptly crashed back down on his face.

"Damn," he muttered, "weak as a kitten. I say, corporal, can you help me to the plane, d'you think?"

Casca lifted him erect, then lay him over his shoulder and carried him to the plane where he placed him feet-first in the rear cockpit. Wothering slumped into the seat, then screamed and came erect again, holding painfully to the sides of the cockpit, his face stark white and pouring sweat from the effort.

"Damn. Won't do at all. Can't sit down with half my bloody arse shot off. I say, d'you expect to use that parachute?"

"Don't even know how to, sir."

"Well, perhaps you could lend it to me, eh?"

With an enormous effort he hauled himself up while Casca stuffed his chute and the remnants of Wothering's ruined one into one side of the cockpit, making a lopsided cushion to keep the officer's mangled butt clear of the seat.

"Yes, I can manage this alright. But I'll leave most of the flying to you, and save the pressure on my busted arse."

"But, sir, I can't fly."

"Nonsense, you're a natural. Besides, the Jerries could be here any minute. Let's get going, shall we?"

Casca walked to the propellor and cranked it around twice. Wothering closed the switch.

"Contact!" he called and on the next turn the motor fired and the propellor became a fast moving blur. With considerable misgiving, but no real alternative, Casca climbed into the observer's seat. The plane was already moving forward. From behind him Casca heard the pilot's cheerful voice.

"We've got about a quarter tank of gas. Plenty of room here for a good long run."

As the plane gathered speed, Casca watched the grass and stones turn to a blur. Up ahead the grazing goats were once more racing about in terror. To Casca's astonishment he found that the pilot was right. Through the stick he could feel the wing surfaces of the plane being lifted by the fast moving air. He eased the stick back just a little, and the ground fell away beneath them.

"Perfect, old bean. Jove, but you're a good flyer. Now I know we came east from our lines to where we spotted those Jerries," he groaned in pain. "Where they spotted us. So, I think we'll weave a sort of zigzag heading back west. Just weave over toward northwest for a bit, and then weave back to the southwest, eh?"

Casca banked slightly, and the plane soared away along the chosen route.

"See anything familiar?" Wothering shouted.

"Farms," Casca answered.

"Yes. It all looks pretty much the same, doesn't it? Let's try the other way for a little."

The flying, Casca discovered, was a delight. He played about in the air like a bird, whooping like an excited schoolboy when a sudden air pocket dropped them toward the ground or a draft of hot air pushed them aloft.

They made a number of passes back and forth, and Casca's anxiety about their petrol supply was beginning to build again when he saw something. He pointed and Wothering swivelled painfully to look.

"Jove!" he exclaimed. "We've found our pot of gold."

Casca wasn't too sure about that. What he had seen rapidly grew larger. This was no mere regiment's HQ, but a huge

military encampment with a number of tents and even some
timber buildings, a few trucks and ambulances, several large
motorcars, half a dozen airplanes, and what was clearly a
huge store of petrol, hundreds of barrels of the stuff. Beyond
the petrol store there was another collection of squat cylin-
drical tanks, but Casca could not guess what they were.

"Climb, then bank right." Wothering spoke just as Casca
was thinking it might be time to get out of sight. As he
responded he reflected that for the moment he had felt in
command of the plane. The authority in Wothering's voice
had reminded him that he was the driver.

"They've probably seen us anyway," the captain said.
"D'you have any of those Mills bombs with you? I hear
you're a dab hand with them."

Casca confirmed that, as usual, he had half a dozen.

"Good, I'll take control. We'll come in low and level,
and you select a target—pick something well ahead. We'll
be going pretty fast, but otherwise it should be about the
same as from a balloon. I'll make one recce pass and then
two more as slow as I can."

Casca roved his eyes over the landscape, but their maneuver to avoid detection had taken them too high to distinguish any of the few distinctive landmarks.

"Let's get down now and take a look-see," Wothering
shouted and turned the nose downward.

The pilot skillfully lost altitude. And as they approached
the camp, they were at about treetop level.

Casca spotted an enormous parade; thousands, tens of
thousands of men were drawn up in ranks, standing
bareheaded in the sun. At the head of the parade a fat priest
was waddling about before a field altar, celebrating holy
Mass to call down from Heaven God's blessing on these
troops who were, Casca guessed, to launch an offensive at
dawn on the morrow. At that time the priest would, no
doubt, be several miles away behind the lines, celebrating
Mass for some nuns in a convent and looking forward to a
nice breakfast of black sausage and sauerkraut.

The plane swept over the massed soldiers who were staring up at the small aircraft. There were so many men, it would be impossible to miss. Casca decided not to wait for Wothering's slow pass and bit the pins from three grenades and dropped them in quick succession.

He saw one fall among the praying men, scattering them in all directions, but it failed to explode. Then altar, priest, and tabernacle all disappeared in a flash of fire and a great cloud of dust. The third grenade exploded in the latrines beyond the parade ground, blowing into the air the broken timbers of the crude sheds along with various bits of the bodies of men who had been hiding there smoking.

"Hey, I say," protested Wothering, "that's hardly cricket, bombing a church parade."

"Judgment from heaven," the Eternal Mercenary said seriously. "If you come back to the right, I'll drop the others on that fuel dump."

Wothering did as Casca asked. Again the first grenade was a dud, but Casca had the satisfaction of seeing the other two explode among the piles of fuel drums, and the high octane petrol burst into flames. As they roared away gaining altitude, Casca looked back and saw more explosions as the fire spread.

CHAPTER TWENTY

"For sure all those men and equipment came along a main road," the pilot shouted. "I'm going to stay low and circle till we find it."

It didn't take long. As Wothering had guessed there was a major road just to the north of the German encampment, and he quickly identified it on his map as *Chemin des Dames*. More German troops were marching east along the road, together with a number of artillery pieces drawn by mules.

Wothering swooped low to inspect the moving army, attracting numerous bursts of rifle fire.

The road ran past several burned-out villages. The slopes of the low hills were a maze of trenches dotted with large shell craters. German Army engineers had hastily thrown bridges across the streams alongside the blackened and broken remains of the old ones that had been dynamited by French army engineers in their withdrawal or destroyed by artillery fire.

The only trees to be seen were charred stumps, and all the houses and barns were flattened ruins, the few standing walls riddled with rifle and machine gun fire. Casca could clearly see broken guns, ammunition carts and ambulances, the bloated bodies of dead horses rotting alongside them. And on the near hills were hastily dug cemeteries, hundreds and hundreds of little white crosses in rows like infantry on parade.

Wothering climbed and set course for the British lines and handed the controls back to Casca announcing casually that he was going to take a little nap. His offhand manner didn't fool Casca who readily guessed that the demands of the brief flying action had reopened his wound and that he was once again faint from the loss of blood.

Wherever he looked, from this height the French countryside all appeared the same. Tiny houses and barns and hay ricks were dotted about the gently undulating landscape. Here and there were small rivers and a few roads that passed through small villages each with a church or two and a town hall.

At last, off to his left, he saw a larger town with bigger buildings. As he turned to shout to Wothering, he spotted a cathedral.

But the pilot was unconscious. Casca unbuckled his harness and stood on his seat to reach into the back cockpit and wake the wounded officer. Wothering's pain-wracked eyes fluttered open, and he struggled upright in his seat. He gulped a mouthful of whisky from his flask and some color returned to his pallid face.

"Ah yes, that'll be Rheims," he mumbled. Our lines are just a few miles south. Now . . ." The rest of what he had to say was drowned out by an enormous backfire as the engine cut out.

"Ah yes," Wothering muttered, "had to happen. Well, just set her down anywhere that looks pretty flat."

For a moment Casca remained standing as he was, staring in amazement at the calm face of the British officer, then he realized that Wothering was about to pass out again, and he dropped back into his seat and turned his attention to seeking someplace that looked flat.

The gently rolling landscape suddenly looked very different, a patchwork of steep hillsides and narrow valleys with scarcely a level patch to be seen—and then only plowed fields.

He chose one and pointed it out.

"Yes, it will have to do," came Wothering's tired voice. "Better buckle up, though. Could be rough on the undercart.

Go around to the east and come back to land right into the
northwest—I think that's where the wind is from.''

The Nieuport was gliding easily, and when Casca turned
they were about forty feet above the ground.

''Now, head for that haystack in the next field,'' Wothering shouted. ''Perfect. Exactly right. Aim to set her down
just over that first stone fence. If you can . . .''

The voice died away, and Casca knew that the officer
had lapsed back into unconsciousness.

The stone fence was coming up, and Casca cleared it
easily then brought up the nose for the stall, but the plane
sailed on down the length of the field.

Casca lifted the nose a little more. It seemed to him that
he had the aircraft standing on its tail, but still they stayed
airborne, moving down the length of the field like a rag
blown on the wind. The stone fence at the farther end of
the field was coming up fast. Then, at last, the Nieuport
started to settle toward the ground. Too late. The fence was
dead ahead.

Casca hauled back on the stick.

The Nieuport reared up and over the stone wall. The
unpowered craft stalled, and the plane dived for the ground.

Casca came to in the cockpit, blood streaming from a
gashed forehead where he had struck the instrument panel.
His back felt like it had been wrenched out of line and one
wrist was certainly sprained if not broken. His head throbbed
unmercifully, and there was a hell of a lot of blood.

He unbuckled his harness and got groggily to his feet.
The rear cockpit was empty. He climbed out onto the wing.
The plane had sheared off the top half of the haystack,
spreading it out over thirty yards, a large part of it pushed
ahead of where the Nieuport had come to rest.

And in the hay scattered ahead of the plane, Casca could
see Wothering lying on his back. He had evidently been
too weak to take his own advice about buckling up.

His eyes opened as Casca reached him. He glanced briefly
around him and smiled wanly. Then he passed out again.

Casca felt him over, but couldn't find any further injuries. He dressed the reopened wound, then bandaged his own head, and sat wearily beside the wounded officer.

Wothering came to again and tried to sit up, sucking in his breath in an agonized gasp as his gashed buttock took his weight. He turned onto his belly and lifted himself on his elbows to look around.

"Hmm. I see you found the haystack alright."

"Yes," Casca answered, "I just couldn't get her down in time."

"My fault," the pilot said. "Should have started the approach farther back. The head doesn't function quite right when it's running short on blood. I see you've lost quite a bit, too."

"Yes." Casca felt the blood still seeping into the bandage around his head. "The flow is slowing now. I'll be alright in a bit."

"Stretch out," Wothering said. "That's an order. I can keep watch for a bit."

Casca didn't feel like arguing. And there was little choice anyway. Neither of them was in any sort of shape to run away—or to fight. Some troops, German for sure, should arrive any minute and take them prisoner. He allowed himself to sink into unconsciousness.

He woke to Wothering's urgent command. "Wake up, Corporal! W've got company coming, and it's not what we expected."

Casca opened his eyes expecting to see a number of field-gray uniformed infantry toting Mauser rifles. What he saw was worse. There were only three gray uniforms, but they were bedecked with gold braid and riding in a large, open Mercedes motorcar.

Behind the wheel of the Mercedes sat a tall, elegant-looking German. But he was no chauffeur—the gold braid and the splendid uniform suggested that he was a high ranking officer if not a royal prince, and the wings on his chest denoted that he was a pilot.

With the agility of an athlete, the driver leaped from his seat, drawing a pistol as he did so. He walked toward the downed airplane casually displaying the Luger. He spoke politely in coarse English, addressing himself to Wothering.

"Good afternoon, Englander. Welcome to the territory of the New Greater Germany. I gather you are wounded and will excuse you from standing."

He ignored Casca, but Casca included himself in the dispensation from standing since his bandaged head bore witness that he too was wounded.

"Allow me to introduce myself. My name is Hermann Goering, and these two gentlemen are my friends, the Baron Von Richtofen and *Oberleutnant* Max Immelmann. We are all flyers on our way to join our squadron. On behalf of all of us, I would like to thank you for a very entertaining spectacle." He laughed heartily.

"Good afternoon," Wothering replied. "I am Captain Henry Osgood Wothering, and this is Corporal Casterton. We are obviously your prisoners, and I accept that. I deny, however, your claim to this part of France. I happen to have read some of the ravings of your Herr Walter Rathenau, and I deny all of his claims."

"I am not surprised," Goering sneered. "From such an inferior pilot I would not expect any high level of intellectual understanding. But let me tell you, our Rathneau is right when he talks of *Lebensraum*. As he puts it: 'We need land on this earth.' "

"Everybody does," Wothering replied, "but that doesn't entitle you to take it from France."

"We have the same right to take it from France as you have to take India, Ireland, or Africa. We are going to build a new German Empire here, 'Mitteleuropa,' and if the French are too stupid to see that it is in their own best interests, then we will just have to show them. A strong, unified central Europe under Germany will be able to stand and compete against the other empires—British, American, and Russian. History demands it, and we are going to accomplish it.

"But we are wasting time. What was the nature of the mission that you so clumsily aborted with your ridiculous landing?"

"We are your prisoners of war," Wothering answered, "and we are not required to give you any information."

"Well, no matter," Goering said. "There is little that we don't already know of the pathetic attempts of your contemptible little army to stand in the way of history. I probably know more of the dispostions and strengths, I should say weaknesses, of your army than you do."

Casca, sitting ignored on the ground, grimaced. The arrogant German was surely right. There was so little left of the British Expeditionary Force that German flyers, who were over the lines daily, doubtless did know more of its circumstances than the British officers did.

"Well, you certainly will not be passing on the information you have gained of our situation. Just leave your weapons on the ground there and get into the car," Goering said.

They got into the rear seat with Immelmann, then Goering pulled the big car around in a tight turn and roared away.

The Mercedes pulled up within the German encampment that they had just bombed, and Captain Wothering was taken to the headquarters building. Casca was marched away to a compound where he joined a small number of other prisoners, French and British, and all enlisted men.

These other prisoners had been captured from scouting parties, or even out of their own lines by raiding parties of German infantry, due to demands from the German high command for intelligence information. That they would risk such raids suggested that there must be a major push imminent. The prisoners had all been intensively interrogated and, Casca guessed, had told the Germans the little they knew.

It seemed scarcely worth the trouble. Nothing significant

had changed in the positons of either army since the Battle of the Marne earlier in the month. Trains were daily rushing French troops to the front as the Germans either knew or should assume. Perhaps there were British reinforcements on the way, but certainly the Tommies in the trenches would know nothing of such movements. With a bored sigh Casca sat down to wait his turn for interrogation.

He was not kept waiting long. To his surprise he was taken before the elegant officer who had found them.

Goering was in a rage. The sneering good humor that he had shown by the downed plane had been replaced by a seething tantrum.

"So, you are the barbarian who bombed our troops at their prayers? And who destroyed our fuel supply?

"When we came upon your plane, we were still on our way here and did not then know of your monstrous attacks."

Goering slammed his fist into the desk with such force that the gold seal ring that he wore on his little finger stamped his emblem into the wood.

"*Himmelherrgott!*" he snarled. "We have plenty of men, and, for that matter, plenty of priests, but you have cost us most of our petrol. It will take us many days to replenish supplies, and our assault upon Verdun cannot be delayed."

Verdun? Casca was puzzled. Verdun was certainly the key sector of the Maginot line. But it was not what he would consider a worthwhile military objective. But he tried to keep the conversation going.

"You will not find Verdun an easy target."

The big German's good humor returned momentarily. "Ach, but you are wrong. You missed what should have been your real target. Had your bombs landed amongst our chlorine store, you might have really damaged our attack. Yes indeed, we are about to teach the French and you British a real lesson at Verdun. You will be totally defeated within a matter of hours. We have a new weapon that is about to completely revolutionize warfare.

"Our victory at Verdun will open the eyes of the French

people to the fact that they have nothing more to hope for. Beyond Verdun there are objectives for which the French General Staff will be compelled to throw into battle every man they have—and the forces of France will bleed to death. On the other hand, should the French withdraw and abandon their splendid fortress to us, the effect on the morale of France will be enormous.''

His manner changed again.

''You dumb fucking corporal, you don't realize just what you have done. You have grounded the world's best three flyers just when the war effort of the fatherland most needs our services.

''Now,'' he waved a long, threatening finger in Casca's face, ''I want to know how you did that?''

''Did what?'' Casca asked innocently.

''Don't play with me, Englander!'' Goering snarled. ''How did you aim your bombs? What special equipment does your plane carry? I have men examining it now, so I will know soon enough anyway. How do you carry these bombs? What sort of bombs are they? And how the hell do you aim them?''

''Just put it down to luck,'' Casca answered.

CHAPTER TWENTY-ONE

"Luck?" Goering's voice was a shrill screech, a comical sound coming from the athletic body in the elegant uniform. "Luck! You dumb Englander corporal. We three, Immelmann, Richtofen, and myself are the three best pilots in the world, and we have not accomplished what you have done here. Don't talk to me of luck. Even from a zeppelin it is difficult to hit a target on the ground, and it flies only at forty miles an hour. You must have been doing twice that speed. Now, you will kindly tell me just how you did it."

Casca looked the German in the eyes. He had no idea of anything that he could possibly say. Luck was the only true explanation, but if the German chose to believe instead that there was some secret, sophisticated weaponry involved, he was certainly not going to tell him otherwise.

But he could think of nothing to say. His mind was totally occupied with what Goering had said. An imminent push on Verdun? And a secret weapon? Chlorine? What the hell sort of weapon uses chlorine? Maybe some machine that runs on it? Impossible, no machine could function with such a corrosive chemical. Does it explode easily? Some new sort of grenade?

Behind Goering's epauletted shoulder there was an open window, and outside Casca could see the huge Mercedes. As his mind raced to try to find something to say that would satisfy the German, he saw two German soldiers escorting Captain Wothering to the car. The late afternoon sun glinted from the bright paintwork, and as he stared at the car, Casca saw another gleam from the cluster of keys in the dashboard.

He was already moving as fast as the thought was forming in his mind. He gathered his legs under him and threw himself across the desk, his outstretched arms reaching for the epauletted shoulders.

The chair went over backwards, and Goering fell, surprised and winded by Casca's weight thudding on top of him. Before the German could recover, Casca was on his feet and then diving headfirst through the open window. He rolled as he hit the ground and came up running.

Ahead of him the two soldiers were loading the wounded officer into the rear seat of the Mercedes with their backs to him. The one he reached first never knew what hit him. Casca's swinging fist took him behind the ear, and he slumped to the ground. The second soldier had a little more time, but it didn't do him any good.

Wothering put all of his diminished strength into an elbow jolt that doubled him over. Instantly, Casca was on the soldier's back, slamming his face over and over again into the quickly bloodied steel panels of the Mercedes until the German's body went limp, and Casca allowed it to fall to the ground.

As Wothering struggled through the open back door, he paused only long enough to retrieve the unconscious soldier's pistol. Casca turned the key and the dashboard instruments lit up. He ran to the front of the car and turned the crank handle.

Nothing happened.

"There's an electric starter," Wothering shouted from where he was still dragging himself into the back seat. "Should be a button on the dashboard."

Casca jumped into the driver's seat and stabbed at a black button. The windshield wipers scraped across the glass.

"On the floor," Wothering's voice said weakly. "Maybe it's on the floor."

Casca looked down. There were two pedals which he was sure were the clutch and the brake, and another that was surely the accelerator. There was also a small, round button. He tramped his foot on it; the motor whirred and instantly fired.

At the same instant he heard the bark of a gun and a bullet passed somewhere nearby. He glanced back toward the hut where he had been interrogated. Goering was leaning out of the small window with the Luger in his hand. A bright orange flash accompanied by the whine of a bullet alerted Casca that the man knew how to shoot.

He looked to his right and saw a number of soldiers running toward the car, cranking their rifles into action as they ran.

"The hell with finesse," he grunted as he engaged what he hoped was first gear and tramped the accelerator to the floor.

The big car shot away at tremendous speed, taking Casca completely by surprise as it hurtled over the uneven ground. He wrestled with the wheel as he looked for something like a road, but the whine of bullets passing close kept his foot to the floor.

He found a rutted cartway and gunned the huge car along it. A quick look to the rear, and he saw that their pursuit was confused and already outdistanced.

A gateway was coming up with a sentry hurrying to open the barrier. He just had time to do so and jumped out of the way saluting smartly as the Mercedes raced through the opening. Casca caught a glimpse of the sentry's startled face as he saw the khaki uniforms. Casca tipped him a salute for his trouble and changed gear, pressing the big car over the rough track as fast as he dared.

He heard a chuckle in his ear. Wothering was leaning on the back of his seat.

"That elegant chappy boasted to me that this is his own private auto," he laughed. "If he ever catches you, he'll fry your hide."

Casca joined in his laughter. "Can you give me any idea where to go?" he asked.

"Not much," Wothering answered. "South and west—

head for the sun is about as close as I can guess. At least we've got the fastest motorcar in Europe. There's no chance that he can catch us.'' After a moment he added, ''Unless he takes to the air.''

They came to a road, and Casca turned onto it—just as they heard the noise of an aircraft engine overhead. A green Fokker biplane was flying the length of the road, and Casca had no doubt that the pilot was Goering. It was quickly evident that he had spotted them. The Fokker climbed and banked, turning tightly so that it was soon behind them.

As it hurtled past overhead the pilot waggled the wings, and Casca heard pistol shots above the sound of the engine. An instant later there was another shot from the back seat of the car as Wothering fired after the departing plane.

Casca glanced at the speedometer. They were moving at more than seventy miles an hour. The big car straddled the narrow road, bouncing about as they struck ruts and potholes and sliding alarmingly as Casca pushed it through corners as fast as he dared.

Then Goering was behind them again, and this time Wothering was ready, the pistol already pointing at the cockpit when the wings dipped and the man between them was exposed. They traded shots, and Wothering fired again as the plane sped away.

''No real chance of damaging the damned thing,'' he grunted in dissatisfaction.

Goering made another pass as they were on a straight stretch of road, almost managing to slow his Fokker to the speed of the car.

For what seemed an age to Casca the plane was overhead and alongside, Wothering's pistol firing rapidly from the back seat. Casca saw the muzzle flash of Goering's pistol, and heard a bullet ricochet from the hood of the car.

Then the plane was ahead of them, and Wothering was firing a last shot at it. On the next pass another bullet hit the car, tearing through the floor close by Casca's feet.

''Damn, but this chappy's good!'' Wothering shouted.

Casca agreed without enthusiasm. If the chase kept up

like this, the German was sooner or later certain to hit one of them or, at least, disable the car.

Goering was now timing his passes to the straight stretches of road, flying slowly at treetop height, and firing two or three shots with each pass. Wothering answered the fire but without effect.

Casca changed tactics and braked almost to a standstill as soon as the Fokker came close so that it swept by quickly. Even so, another shot tore through the upholstery of the back seat.

Then Casca saw an encampment and left the road, heading for where the French tricolor was flying. They were almost to the barbed wire when a French machine gun opened fire on them.

At almost the same instant the Fokker swept overhead, and there was the ring of lead on steel as another of Goering's shots struck the car.

Wothering stood erect, displaying his British khaki uniform, and holding his hands high in the air. The only effect was that more French soldiers opened fire with their rifles.

Then the Fokker was overhead again, but now Casca couldn't brake as this would make them too easy a target for the French soldiers. He kept his foot down, and he heard shot after shot exchanged between the German pilot and his passenger. Mercifully, the French turned their attention to the plane, and Goering banked steeply away as he flew into their fire.

Then the plane was gone, and the French machine gunner was turning his weapon once more toward the Mercedes. Wothering again stood up, his hands raised in the air to demonstrate his inhostility.

The machine gun stopped firing, but now dozens of rifles were trained on them as Casca brought the car to a stop. A number of French soldiers came running toward them, their rifles pointed nervously.

Casca, too, got to his feet and put his hands in the air.

CHAPTER TWENTY-TWO

They were interrogated by a French *chef de batalion*, Commandant Jacques Campion. He was obsessively suspicious and believed that they were German agents. Their arrival in the high-powered sports car persuaded him that they were high ranking German officers.

He refused to be impressed by Wothering's protestations that he had seen for himself that the German plane was pursuing them and firing at them. He was infuriated when Wothering, explaining that he did not know the language, declined to speak with him in German.

He regarded Wothering's command of French as a proof of his Germanness. Nor was he impressed by their command of English as he did not speak the language and held it in contempt. And he adamantly refused to transport them to a British camp, insisting that they were Germans and his prisoners and that the matter did not concern the British.

Wothering then tried telling him that he had urgent military intelligence for the British High Command and demanded that he be taken to General Headquarters.

"So," the Frenchman sneered as if his deepest suspicions had been confirmed, "you admit being in possession of military secrets. Then, as an officer in an army of the Triple Entente, you must reveal this information to me, your superior officer."

Wothering patiently explained that he could under no circumstances do that, as he was not within the French chain of command.

"But if you will just escort me to British Headquarters, we can resolve this whole matter in a moment," he said.

Casca could see that this conversation was never going to get anywhere, and decided to take a hand. He shouted to the astonished Wothering, "*Himmeldonnerwetter! Halt's maul!*"

The French major laughed. "So, the British corporal is telling a British captain to hold his tongue. And in German! What have we here?"

Casca continued to act like a superior officer infuriated by the conduct of an inferior. He hissed at Wothering in the perfect German of a Prussian officer.

"You fool. If that British Major Cartwright near Rheims spots you, he will know what's afoot, and we will have lost the whole game."

"And who is this Major Cartwright?" demanded the French commandant.

Casca glared at him insolently. "We have nothing further to say to you, and will be very content to be your prisoners for the time being."

"For the time being? So, a German attack is imminent, and you hope to be rescued. Well, you are spies, wearing stolen uniforms, so there will be no rescue. I intend to shoot you as spies suspected of espionage."

Casca nodded. "As you like. I don't give a damn what you do."

Wothering could not understand a word of the conversation in German, but he discerned that Casca had an objective clear in his mind, and he smiled at the game.

The sight of what he believed to be two senior German officers grinning at the prospect of a firing squad unnerved the Frenchman. He shouted some orders, and a minute later they were again in the Mercedes, this time with a tricolor pennant flying at the cowl and with an escort of four French soldiers.

Half an hour later they were talking with Major Cartwright, and the sadly discomfited French officer was on his way to his own headquarters with the warning of an imminent attack on Verdun and the proposed use of a new weapon that somehow utilized chlorine.

The attack on the French fortress came at dawn on September twenty-second. As a result of Casca's information, the French army rushed every available man to Verdun, the key strongpoint which was supposed to be impregnable. The British Expeditionary Force had shrunk so much that they held only twenty-one miles of line while the French held more than four hundred miles, the Western Front now running almost from the Belgian coast to the border of Switzerland. But every English soldier who could be spared was rushed to Verdun too, and Major Cartwright's men were allocated to the forward defense of the star-shaped Fort Douaumont.

The attack commenced with the usual predawn artillery barrage which started at first light. The Tommies had been standing to since three o'clock and were ready for action. Many of the shells were what the Tommies called coal boxes—high explosive shells with an impact fuse that detonated the explosive charge when the shell struck the ground or any hard object, releasing great clouds of dense, black smoke. The barrage was still continuing when the first wave of chlorine gas reached the foremost trenches forming the first line of defense of the French fort.

The gas came rolling in dirty, yellow-gray clouds, mixing with the early morning ground mist and the black smoke from the coal-box shells. Behind the rolling clouds Casca could see German soldiers carrying large cannisters of the gas.

Casca's eyes burned, his nose was on fire. The inside of his mouth and his throat felt as if he had been drinking petrol. And with each eddy of the light wind, the clouds of gas rolled closer, and men started to fall, retching and heaving in agony.

It was impossible to stand before this weapon. The British line broke. Officers and men clambered out of the trenches and ran for the fort. Thousands of Germans charged from behind the gas clouds and within minutes were in control of the British trenches with scarcely a shot fired.

But in another minute, they too were running. As the scalding gas clouds enveloped them and scorched the linings of their lungs, they fled in all directions, some running back into the advancing gas clouds only to again turn back and run uselessly about in the area between the defensive trenches and the walls of the fort.

The British made a stand outside the walls, and their sustained rifle fire cut heavily into the confused Germans who were also taking heavy fire from the fort's machine guns.

The wind had died, and the heavy gas lay coiled in clouds close to the ground. The advancing Germans could not get through it, and those who tried to retreat found it blocking their way.

Then the wind sprang up again, but this time blowing out of the south and toward the German lines. The entire German assault was engulfed in the poisonous cloud, and the attack broke up.

But the British were in no shape to counterattack. Almost every man was disabled to some extent, hundreds had been blinded, and many were dying where they lay, their lungs so severely damaged that they had ceased functioning. Only the wind change had saved the force from total annihilation.

By midmorning the gas had dissipated, and the suffering Tommies moved back into their trenches.

German airplanes were playing about in the sky, monitoring the movements on the ground. Casca recognized Goering's Fokker and chanced a shot at it, but without effect.

The Germans soon came again, the gas blowing ahead of them as they neared the British trenches. The wind was now just a series of light eddies which blew the gas first one way, and then the other.

The chlorine devastated the British and then the Germans in turn. The attackers found that they could not get through the gas to take the trenches, and light southerly gusts blew the corrosive chemical back upon them in murderous clouds, forcing the second wave of attackers to turn in frantic retreat without firing a single shot.

The day wore away with men collapsing and dying on both sides. From time to time the gas clouds would clear for a while, and the battle would revert to the pattern that had obtained since the war had started—the attackers dying in droves at the barbed wire entanglements as they ran into sustained machine gun fire from the trenches.

By the end of the day, some two thousand French and British had been killed or severely wounded, and the Germans had lost about the same number, many of them hanging on the wire before the trenches where they had been cut down by machine gun fire from the fort.

Hundreds of men from both sides were blinded and shambled about in no-man's-land, whimpering in pain and confusion.

"This is not the sort of war I care much for," Casca said to Hugh.

The big Welshman stared at him through reddened eyes. "You've been to war before?" he asked.

Casca gritted his teeth. "Not if this is war."

CHAPTER TWENTY-THREE

The stretcher bearers brought in hundreds of gassed men, but there were hundreds more out in the dark forest beyond the trenches. Throughout the night they could be heard coughing, gasping, and vomiting. The autumn night was cold, and there was a freezing wind out of the north that carried with it the chill of the arctic ice. Gradually, the noise died down as the men died, but there were still many of them groaning and calling weakly for help when the troops were stood to at midnight to await the morning's attack.

Everybody was still suffering some ill effect from the gas. Men's faces had been scalded a dirty yellow, the skin peeling away in strips. Their lungs were clogged with the corrosive chemical, their throats and noses scorched.

"Do you think they'll use that gas again?" somebody said.

"Only if they're crazy," another soldier replied. "It did as much harm to them as it did to us. Thank God for that wind change."

"Yeah. Listen, I can hear a German voice now."

From out of no-man's-land came a despairing groan between mumbled words. "*Heilige Maria, Mutter Gottes, erbarme dich unser.*"

"What the hell's he saying?"

"Holy Mary, Mother of God, have pity on us," Casca answered. To the dying German he shouted, "*Behüt euch Gott*—God preserve you!"

"Everything smells of mustard," Cockney Dave said. "I

was dreaming of mince pies. Riding me bicycle down our street I was, which is funny, 'cos I never had one. All down the street chimneys were smoking, and as I passed the houses, I could smell the coal fires. Then I was turning into my house, and my mum was opening the door. I could smell the polishing wax on the floors, and I could smell some hot mince pies—and then they were waking me up, and my nose was full of this rotten mustard smell. If I'd had just one more minute I would have had a nice, hot mince pie for breakfast.''

''Well,'' Hugh Evans laughed, ''there's one good thing about fighting alongside frogs—we do get some sort of breakfast that's worth eating.''

''Yeah, makes a change from our slops, don't it?''

They were eating chunks of cold, cooked bacon with hard French bread and washing it down with strong black coffee.

The artillery bombardment started at four a.m. and continued until dawn when the first field-gray uniforms appeared through the ground mist, and the British and French machine guns opened up on them.

This morning the wind was strongly from the south, and there was no more of the mustard gas. Casca hoped that he would never see it again. The mighty secret weapon had certainly not worked on its first trial. But he had an idea that the weapon would not be scrapped. With the right wind conditions it could be devastating.

The first wave of Germans died by hundreds before they got anywhere near the wire, and by midmorning the attack had diminished to small skirmishes.

Then suddenly there was thunderous noise, and a thousand horsemen were charging into the guns. Each cavalryman had a saber in his hand, a lance in its socket, and a carbine slung across his back.

For the machine guns the horses made even better targets than men, and they were soon dying all over the field. Their dismounted riders formed ranks and poured concerted fire at the British gunners.

Some of the machine guns stopped firing, but when the Germans charged, they were stopped at the first of the wire entanglements, and while they tried to cut through it, the French machine guns from the walls of the fort chopped them to pieces.

These men were tough and well trained, and few of them ran. Most of them used their dead horses for cover and maintained heavy fire with their carbines. From behind them a wave of infantry attacked, and aided by the effective fire of the cavalrymen, many of them made it to the wire. But few got through it.

Twice they did manage to dislodge the Tommies, but their attacks faltered as they approached the walls of the fort and came under concentrated fire from the French defenders. In dogged counterattacks, fighting mainly with bayonets, the Tommies regained their positions.

At the end of the second day, the British were retired to the fort, and French troops took over the forward trenches.

Cockney Dave was far from impressed with the French fort and declared that he would rather be back in the trench.

''What a rotten stink!'' he complained as his nose took in the accumulated odors of sweat, blood, vomit, urine, gun oil, cordite, and the dull odor of spent lead.

The fort was indeed almost impossible to take. Its star shape thrust its points out in all directions, dominating the forest from its hilltop elevation of more than a thousand feet. The walls were concrete, dug into the hill, and more than eight feet thick. And it was well protected with steel-fronted gun turrets.

The wind overnight was out of the northwest, sweeping down from the north pole. The steel gun turrets had frosted over, and the inside walls were thick with ice. It was impossible to sleep, and the gunners were on their feet all night, stamping their boots on the concrete floors as they tried to keep from freezing.

Again the action started before first light. From inside

the massive fortress the artillery fire was less terrifying than in the trenches but seemed even louder.

"What I wouldn't give for just one minute's splendid silence," Cockney Dave groaned.

Casca nodded grim agreement.

His ears were saturated with noise. From the distance came the sound of the German guns followed by the whine of incoming shells and then the explosions as they struck the ground or the walls of the fort. From inside the fort the big French guns fired shot after shot, each resounding explosion followed without interval by another, each shot building on the noise of the previous one to create a vast, unceasing thunder.

This continuous background of noise was augmented by the staccato chatter of machine guns, rifle shots, and the explosions of grenades and punctuated by the screams of men.

Within this ghastly orchestration men spoke little, communicating mainly by signs. Orders came in hoarse screams which were rarely heard and never understood. Only the shrieks of the wounded and the groans of the dying had the power to attract conscious attention.

These were the only sounds. No birds sang; there were no cows or pigs or chickens. The tethered horses and mules were as quiet as the men cowering near them. Any conversation consisted of gasped expletives and shouted curses.

Cockney Dave summed it up: "Hell on the ears, ain't it?"

Not too good on the eyes either, Casca thought as he stared out at no-man's-land where the shape of the tortured landscape was emerging with the dawn. What had once been a forest of splendid trees was now a tangle of splintered trunks without branches, buds or flowers. The ground was churned into thousands of shell craters and abandoned, half-dug foxholes. Grotesquely erect bodies stood grinning, entangled in the wire.

The battle lasted for four days, and the Hotchkiss machine

guns seemed to firè almost nonstop, pouring lead into the waves of attacking Germans, brass cartridge cases spewing from their breeches.

More than ten thousand men died, but the Germans got no closer to the fort than the forward trenches.

Meanwhile, for five days another battle raged nearby at Picardy, and a few days later came the Battle of Artois. In total, nearly thirty thousand men died, and the only result was that the Germans took St. Mihiel and some small and strategically unimportant villages on the left bank of the Meuse River.

On October first, a strong German force under Hans von Beseler attacked Antwerp, and after nine days of endless slaughter, forced the Belgian and British defenders to evacuate.

There began a race for the seas that the Germans won. They took Ghent, Bruges, and Ostend in a murderous five days.

Then the Belgians flooded the whole of the Yser district, and as autumn turned to winter men and mules found themselves up to their knees in freezing swamps. The Germans took Lille and attacked southeast of Ypres in an action that lasted almost a month and produced no result at all.

On December fourteenth, the Allies launched a general attack on the whole front from Nieuport to Verdun. The action lasted for ten days producing tens of thousands of casualties with no gain.

All but a tip of Belgium was in German hands, and they held one tenth of France including ten thousand square miles of coal and iron mines.

The war that was to have been over by Christmas was now almost half a year old with no end in sight.

CHAPTER TWENTY-FOUR

The hard freezes of November and December had once signalled the end of what military strategists had called the campaigning season, and troops moved into winter quarters, cantonments where they passed the days in training for the campaigns that would commence at the end of the spring rains in April.

Casca's mind ran back over many of the European campaigns he had taken part in—in the time of the Caesars, of Charlemagne, Crecy in the fourteenth century and Agincourt in the fifteenth during the Hundred Years' War, the campaigns of Charles in the sixteenth, the Thirty Years' War in the seventeenth century, the Seven Years' War in the eighteenth. Never had he experienced campaigning in the depths of winter.

Nor could he see any sense in it now.

The two enormous armies were entrenched opposite each other for hundreds of miles. Every day tens of thousands of men raced into the muzzles of the machine guns, and thousands of them died. But no significant territory had changed hands since Antwerp at the beginning of October, and outside Belgium, most of the war had been fought back and forth over the same ten miles or less, all the way along almost five hundred miles of front.

But the high command on both sides still dreamed of a quick victory, now pinning their faith in the new weapons that were being developed. Their faith remained undimmed although most of these brilliant new developments—the airplane and zeppelin, radio telegraph and field telephone, bicycle detachments, poisonous gas—had so far proved of dubious worth in the field.

Christmas Eve found Casca and what was left of the Old Contemptibles back in the trenches near Rheims. Captain George had been busted back to lieutenant a couple of times, Major Cartwright was now a colonel, and Hugh Evans a sergeant. Casca was still a corporal, and Cockney Dave still a private.

Unending warfare had become the normal condition of life. The men in the trenches were coming to believe that the fighting might never end. They lived in a world of endless fear, amidst blood, sweat, piss, shit, vomit, and tears. The cold brought misery, fog, rain, sleet, snow, hail, and mud. Miles and miles of freezing mud, knee deep in the no-man's-land that had been exploded, dug up, and exploded more every day for almost six months.

The roads had turned to rivers of sluggish mud that drifted between steep and slippery banks. Movement was almost impossible but was ordered every day by the commanders of one side or the other.

The trenches were a filthy, stinking mess of lice, leeches, ticks, fleas, rats, mice, cockroaches, and what had started out as men.

The lines had settled down into semipermanent communities, a network of holes in the ground, connected by communication trenches, linked to dugouts, backed by duckboarded latrines, dirty cookhouses with their greasy cooks, everlasting mess lines, and uneatable food. Casca thought back over almost twenty centuries of campaigning, and his memory came up with no experience as miserable.

His long life had been spent in an endless series of army huts and canvas tents occasionally interspersed with hotel rooms and even a few palaces. Only a very few times had he known what might be called a home with a wife and friends, a horse, a cow, a dog. But never for long, and never with the joyful scamper of children around the hearth.

He had learned to envy men whose lives were short but whose seed might survive forever. His own seed, like his blood, was poisoned by the curse of the Nazarene. Even though he had experienced much and learned a great deal, he could never pass on his knowledge to his progeny.

But now he found that he felt sorry for his comrades who had once led normal lives. The continous hell of life in the trenches was as intolerable an existence as he had ever experienced, but for men who had left homes and families, such a life must be an unbearable agony.

Once in a long while there was mail from home—often as worrying for family men as their own desperate existence at the front. The blockades had carried the war into the homes of the civilian population. Another front had been added—the Home Front. Everything was in short supply on the home front; people were working longer hours and spending more and more of their time in the eternal queues to buy sugar or flour, a pair of shoes, or razor blades.

Rumors were rife—confusing and contradictory, they were traded back and forth in the trenches and even with the enemy in shouted conversations with lookouts in the opposing lines which were now sometimes only a hundred yards apart.

"We're moving out." "We're moving up." "We're moving back." "A big push." "A major retirement." "Reinforcements are on the way."

"Ah, the hell with it," Cockney Dave cursed. "The only rumor we don't hear is that we're stayin' here—and that's all that ever happens."

The endless siege of the entrenched enemies went on in defiance of all military logic—and contrary to common sense. Suffering, pain, and useless sacrifice became the normal life of men on both sides. The warrior legend was fast losing any romance or glory.

The marks of combat were showing in the hollow eyes of men whose eyes had become focussed in the notorious two-thousand-yard stare.

More and more men were coming out of the line un-
wounded but no longer fit for battle. Shell shocked troops
were everywhere, mumbling, whispering, crying, or just
shaking and shivering. Some men went into a state of terror
as their friends died alonside them and then slipped into a
torpor from which they could not be roused.

Nothing worked with these men. Some of the doctors
called them "casualties of the spirit" and tried to treat them
kindly. Others shouted at them: "Malingerer! Quitter! Coward!"

The French shot them after drum-head court-martials, but
still the disease continued to spread. And it was the same
in all the armies.

The Red Cross distributed Christmas parcels, cough
medicines, and uplifting tracts from the Bible. Most of the
men were unimpressed, and many did not even open the
packages, although some of them contained the wine and
cheese they had dreamed of for months.

Shortly after sunset on Christmas Eve, the desultory artillery fire died down. One after another the machine guns
fell silent, and then the sporadic rifle fire died away. A
strange silence settled over the front.

Captain George leaped out of the trench and up onto its
mound of earth, ignoring the warning shouts of his friends.

From out of the swirling winter ground mists solid figures
were beginning to appear. The German army was advancing
on the British lines. But this advance was like no other that
anybody had ever experienced. There was no barrage, not
even a rifle shot. The only sound was the faintly musical
chant: *"Kamerad. Kamerad."*

"What the hell does that mean? *Kamerad?* Comrade? Is
that what they're saying?"

The field-gray uniforms could now be clearly seen through
the gray mist. Every man seemed to be carrying something,
but none of their burdens were weapons.

Then the boy officer saw something he recognized—a
goose. A giant German *Feldwebel* was holding it aloft by

the neck; his other raised arm held two bottles. All along the slowly advancing line the young Scot could now discern men wearing bandoliers of sausages, carrying armfuls of cake, bottles of wine, Red Cross parcels. The German soldiers were plodding determinedly through the mud, walking into the British guns, laden with Christmas presents and protected only by the one word: *kamerad*.

Captain George turned to shout down into the trench, "Corporal, pass me the wire cutters and some of those comfort parcels."

The corporal, trained to obey any order, handed up the tool, a bottle of Guinness stout, and a Christmas pudding. George took them from him and jumped down from the mound to start snipping through the coils of barbed wire.

The amazed corporal watched as his officer dropped the wire cutters into the mud and walked out into no-man's-land through the opening he had made in the wire.

The Scot and the German met and fell into each other's arms like long lost brothers, the goose dangling down the young officer's back as the German enfolded him in a great hug.

Then the two men were sitting in the mud, and George was biting the cap from the beer bottle.

"What's goin' on out there?" Cockney Dave demanded from within the trench.

"Damned if I know," the corporal replied. "Pass me some of those bottles, will you?" He filled his arms and jumped to the ground, running through the opening in the wire.

All along the line the same thing was happening. Within minutes the British trench was full of Germans, each with his arm around a Tommy's shoulder and a bottle in his hand.

Yuletide, Casca remembered in a rush. A pagan festival that predated the birth of Christ by some thousands of years. A time of peace—even the ever war-ready German tribesmen of antiquity had realized that there was no sense in fighting in the snow. So they turned the very depth of winter into a time of peace, forgiveness, and gift giving. It was a time when even the worst enemies could break bread together, even feast mightily in each other's homes while they joked and made light of their differences and disputes.

And Casca recalled that when Germany was eventually Christianized, the people had accepted the new religion but had refused to give up this midwinter festival. Now it seemed the festival was to survive even in the midst of mechanized war.

The party lasted all night.

At dawn the Germans started to leave for their own lines, but at noon there were still some sleeping drunkenly in the British trenches.

The rumor mill said that the same thing had happened all the way along the hundreds of miles of front, from the North Sea to Switzerland. Some said that even the senior officers had been entertaining each other in their dugouts. Certainly nothing was said about the massive, collective indiscipline, and the guns were silent all through Christmas Day.

CHAPTER TWENTY-FIVE

December twenty-sixth dawned red and bloody.

The Tommies had been standing to since two o'clock, and at four every big gun commenced firing.

Within seconds answering shots were heard, and high explosive shells were bursting all around the British lines. The Tommies were ordered over the top, and they clambered out, running forward through the exploding shells.

Fifty yards into no-man's-land they met an advancing horde of Germans, and as the sun came up, it lit them as they butchered each other with rifle fire, bayonets, and bare hands.

Both the British and the German artillery were pouring shells into the area, and machine gunners from both sides were spraying the embattled troops with lead. At such close quarters the gunners were killing as many of their own as they were of the enemy.

But the battle raged on. It seemed as if everybody, from the high command to the gunners to the privates in the line had lost their senses. Successive waves of infantry poured out from both sides, and the number of men struggling and dying grew by the hour.

The carnage continued throughout the day, and when darkness brought something akin to sanity, Casca learned that the action had been recorded as a "brisk engagement," which in the language of the high command meant fifty per cent casualties.

One, Casca was appalled to learn, was Captain George.

He had, as usual, led repeated charges with his beloved bagpipes, with Harry, his drummer boy, beside him, their red jackets and tartan kilts standing out clearly among the khaki uniforms. Harry had collected a bullet through the throat, and while trying to effect a dressing on the wound in the heat of the furious battle, George had fallen to a German bayonet.

The next morning the battle was rejoined, but this time the British troops were strictly on the defensive. Most of the artillery and almost all of the machine guns had expended all of their available ammunition in the frenzy of the previous day. The Tommies had to crouch in their trenches throughout the early morning barrage that did not cease until the attack by the German infantry came so close that they were running into the shells from their own guns.

The artillery fire rolled away, but the Germans had developed a new technique and had hauled with them a number of Maxim machine guns with drum magazines which could be operated by one man. The heavy guns had their water cooling hoses detached and could fire almost a thousand rounds before the water in the cooling jacket began to boil.

They were now able to set up these guns on bipods just outside the British wire and pour concentrated fire directly into the British trenches where the defending machine guns were silent for lack of ammunition.

It was impossible to face such fire, and the Tommies abandoned their trenches, retreating to the next line of prepared positions. The Germans could not chase them with their heavy, red-hot, steaming machine guns, and the Tommies had a small respite.

But not for long.

The Germans recommenced their artillery fire, concentrating on the new positions and laying down such a barrage that the Tommies suffered enormous casualties. Later in the day the Germans again brought up their portable machine guns, and by nightfall another ''brisk engagement'' was recorded.

That night Casca found Cockney Dave and asked him if he knew anything of Captain George's death.

"Yeah," Dave said, "George is not too far away."

"You know where his body lies?"

Dave jerked his head toward no-man's-land. "He's out there."

"Unburied?" Casca sat up with a jerk.

"Yeah. I thought about bringing him in when I found him, and then later I thought of going back for him with a stretcher and a burial detail. We can do that if you like."

First light the next morning found a stretcher detail of Casca, Hugh, Cockney Dave, and some others out in no-man's-land, looking down into a shell crater.

Captain George's face grinned up at them, the lips pulled back in a last grimace that death had softened into a smile. He had one arm around the shoulder of the drummer boy, and their pipes and drum were beside them. The German on whose bayonet he had died was lying on top of him, the point of George's bayonet protruding from his back.

"How old were they?" Hugh asked.

"Maybe sixteen," Casca answered. "Harry might be younger."

In the freezing wind the bodies had not yet begun to decay.

"This is where they grew up, ain't it?" Cockney Dave said. "They wouldn't want to lie in that military cemetery, all lined up with they don't know who, like being on parade in a strange battalion. But out here, why, they're amongst friends—their own kind—front-line soldiers."

"Yes, you're right," Casca answered. "This is their place alright."

They returned to the trenches with the stretchers empty.

During the night some ammunition wagons had come up, and they were able to withstand the day's attack. But the casualties were still enormous, and Hugh Evans died in one of the murderous onslaughts of the portable Maxim guns.

The opposing lines were now so close that the Germans had developed a technique for effective rifle fire from trench to trench. They used a small telescope fitted over the sights of their Mausers, and their marksmen could hit any Tommy who was incautious enough to show his head above the earthworks. Striking a match to light a cigarette became especially dangerous. Matches were scarce and precious, but no longer did several men take a light from one match. A German marksman only needed the time it took to light two cigarettes to aim his rifle. To light a third cigarette had become suidical. And not a few men died shouting: "Put out that light!"

Some of the surviving Old Contemptibles had served in India and had developed and sharpened the necessary skills for hunting snipe, a small, fast bird, and the favorite game fowl of the British in India. These marksmen, called snipers, were posted on the earthworks to answer the threat of the German sharpshooters.

Winter dragged on. Actions were attempted in the freezing mud and snow, and there were huge casualties on both sides, but no territory changed hands.

The battalion was thrown into a mid-February attack on the German entrenchments in the eastern Champagne district.

The German line had been impregnably strengthened. They had made a catacomb of the hills overlooking the Allied trenches. Dugouts had been timbered with huge beams and reinforced with concrete. There were underground arsenals, aid stations, gun repair shops, even laundries.

Day after day for weeks the combined British and French force attempted to dislodge the Germans, and when after six weeks the attack was called off, they had not yielded so much as a foxhole in return for some thirty thousand Allied casualties.

A ragged copy of *The Times* appeared in the British trenches. It reported an eloquent speech in which Lloyd George had praised the troops for their ascent of "the glittering peaks of sacrifice," and also announced the doubling of the income tax from ninepence to a shilling and sixpence per pound. Turkey had entered the war on the side of the Central Powers. There were reinforcements of a quarter of a million men ready to leave England for France, and contingents from the British dominions were on their way. The newspaper also castigated the lack of ammunition for the British forces that had become a major scandal with threats of a change of government in London.

The paper also had a headline: FIRST GREAT AIR RAID IN HISTORY. A number of British planes had taken off from Dover and Dunkirk and bombed a power station, a sailing ship, harbor warehouses, a railway station, transport on the Ghistelles Road, and a boat towing some barges. The surprise attacks panicked the civilian victims, resulting in evacuations and work stoppages. Five of the twenty-one planes did not return.

Life in the trenches got worse every day. When the troops were not being uselessly sacrificed in hopeless assaults on the entrenched Germans, their time was spent in boredom, digging latrines, cleaning each other of lice, and freezing in the damp and the Arctic wind.

Cockney Dave went west in one more hopeless attack on the German fortress. Casca was leading his squad in a charge, and they had made it almost to the wire when a Maxim that had remained silent suddenly opened fire right in front of them. Dave fell backwards into a shell crater, and Casca tumbled down beside him.

"Comes as a surprise," Cockney Dave said in wonder. "Funny, ain't it? Shouldn't be no surprise, but somehow it is. Make sure that little widder gets me final pay, will you?" He gave a tired, resigned smile and died.

Casca stood up so that his head was about level with the lip of the crater. Slowly and carefully he fired shot after shot until he killed the whole of the machine gun crew. "Nothing personal," he muttered as he lined up each man in his sights and deliberately squeezed the trigger.

Then he was up and running for the wire, tugging the

pins from Mills bombs. He lobbed the grenades into the wire entanglements and was running through the blasted gap before the smoke had cleared, dropping two more grenades into the trench. He made it into the trench and moved along it, shooting from the hip, as the few survivors of his squad followed behind him.

They had cleared quite a length of the trench when they encountered a determined group of Germans armed with a new chemical weapon, the *Flamenwerfer*.

Casca was in the lead, and was sprayed with the thick, blazing fuel. His clothes and hair ignited, his skin turned to charcoal. He dropped to the floor of the trench, huge chunks of his skin cracking away to expose the bleeding flesh beneath.

His men turned and ran, and the Germans ran after them.

Casca, near death, lay still in the bottom of the trench, but his mind was racing. He seemed to be looking at the battle from above, as if he were in a balloon. He saw his body lying in the mud, surrounded by dead comrades and dying Germans.

"Well, so much for this war," he thought, "I'm glad to be out of it—senseless fucking charade."

Then he was watching a parade of all the men he had known who had died in these fields, from Captain George to the brave fool Major Blandings. They were moving away toward the distant hills but with their faces turned toward him as if waiting for him to join them. Cockney Dave was bringing up the rear, and he turned back to salute and smile. And he saw another procession of horror-struck faces and mangled bodies, and he recognized the men that he had killed in this war.

He had no doubt that he was dying, and the ancient curse of the Nazarene no longer seemed to relate to him. Almost two thousand years of fighting vanished from his memory, crowded out by the enormous numbers of men he head seen die since he had landed in France less than a year ago.

Somebody threw a grenade, and it exploded a few yards

beyond Casca's head. Some empty ammunition crates absorbed the shrapnel but not the concussion, and he slipped into merciful unconsciousness.

He was still unconscious the next day when, at last, the British succeeded in taking the trench from the Germans.

A Tommy stretcher team carried him back to the field hospital where a doctor was about to pronounce him dead when he realized that the exposed red flesh was maintaining its color.

"I don't know what's happening here," he muttered, "but I can't count him off as dead while his metabolism is still functioning. There's nothing I can do for him, though. Just put him aside until he dies."

The next day Casca was still alive, although the doctor could not detect either heartbeat or breathing. But the torn red meat was clearly still hanging onto life, so he had the incinerated body bandaged to keep it clean and again set it aside.

A conference of doctors agreed that Casca was not quite dead, and as there was nothing else they could think to do, they listed him to be repatriated to England.

"It's only a matter of where he's to be buried, but if he's still in this state when he gets to the boat, he might even make it home to be put in the ground."

CHAPTER TWENTY-SIX

When the ambulance train arrived at the coast, Casca's body had still not commenced to rot, so it was loaded with a number of other drastically wounded onto a small freighter, the *Shropshire Maid*, that was sailing for Southampton.

It was a fine spring night with a bright moon in a cloudless sky. Casca with a number of other wounded was placed on deck, lashed to the deck cargo of crates of oranges.

The little ship was contributing mightily to Britain's war effort, running supplies from England to France, and returning with wounded men and cargoes of food. The owner and captain was also getting extremely rich in this process and willing to run the submarine blockade.

Until November of 1914, the U-boat policy had been to board intercepted vessels, allow the crew time to take to the boats, and then sink the ship. In February of 1915, however, the German government declared the waters surrounding Great Britain to be a military area and announced that henceforth enemy merchantmen found in this area would be sunk without warning. This announcement followed the Allies' infringement of international law in November when they had similarly declared the North Sea a military area in the enforcement of their blockade of German ports.

Captain Jacobsen was not concerned unduly. His ship was small and unimportant and was registered in Liberia.

But a submarine commander, Hauptman Wolfgang von Ritter, was almost at the end of his seventeen-day mission and had not yet made a kill. He decided not to risk a miss and the waste of a torpedo by trying for an attack while submerged. He brought his ship to the surface and approached the unarmed merchantman.

Jacobsen's crew were keeping a sharp, seamanlike lookout, but they did not see the black U-boat on the black sea. The first they knew of its presence was a great explosion as the submarine's cannon scored a direct hit near the bow.

The crew raced to the davits and tried to crank down the two heavy lifeboats that were carried on either side of the superstructure. The ship was listing heavily to port where it had been hit, and the starboard side boat proved impossible to launch. The port side boat was dangling in the air when the second cannon shell hit, blasting another hole in the hull and opening it wide to the sea.

In a matter of minutes the ship was sinking beneath the waves, a handful of crew members and a few of the wounded soldiers swimming for their lives until they tired in the cold water.

EPILOGUE

When, an hour later, another British ship came upon the floating wreckage, the crew found only the wounded soldiers floating on the orange crates. They hauled them on board, but none showed any sign of life.

This freighter, the *H.M.S. Abyrton*, was on an urgent mission carrying war materiel and a few troops. The captain wanted to get clear of the submarine-infested waters as quickly as he could. He rang the engine room telegraph for full speed ahead and put the matter of the corpses on his deck out of mind.

There was no time to heave to for a decent burial service, and the captain read a few hasty words from a Bible as the weighted bodies were thrown back into the sea from the moving ship.

The burial detail was startled to find that Casca's body was still warm despite its time in the cold sea.

Concussed, his skin burned to charcoal, and nearly drowned, Casca was yet kept alive by the curse of the prophet he had executed two thousand years earlier.

"Captain, I think this man may be alive," the bo's'n said.

"Well, just as well we didn't throw him over. He sure isn't very alive, though, is he?"

"No, sir. I suppose he'll die soon enough."

"Well, we'll have to carry him along with us until he does die, and we'll put him over the side then. We can't stop to put him ashore, bo's'n. We have our orders for Gallipoli."

CASCA

THE ETERNAL MERCENARY
By Barry Sadler